Street of Blood

Written and Performed
by
Ronnie Burkett

A RIVER BOOK

Published by: River Books
an imprint of The Books Collective
214-21, 10405 Jasper Avenue
Edmonton, Alberta, Canada T5J 3S2
river@bookscollective.com

The Books Collective acknowledges the support of the Canada Council for the Arts for our publishing programme. We also acknowledge the assistance of the Edmonton Arts Council.

Editors for the press: Timothy J. Anderson and Candas Jane Dorsey.

Cover design: Cheryl Anne Lieberman.

Photographs: All photographs by Trudie Lee except pp. i and 61 by Bruce Monk.

Interior typeset by Ana M. Anubis of Ingénieuse Productions, Edmonton, in *Lucida* & *Lucida Sans*, designed and produced by Kris Holmes and Charles Bigelow in 1985, and Hat Nguyen's *Droplet*.

Printed in Canada by Priority Printing, Edmonton.

1 2 3 4 5 05 04 03 02 01

National Library of Canada Cataloguing in Publication Data

Burkett, Ronnie, 1957—
Street of blood

A puppet play.
ISBN 1-895836-87-5

I. Title.
PS8553.U639S77 2002 C812'.6 C2002-910877-2
PR9199.4.B87S77 2002

Cast of Characters

EDNA RURAL, a prairie widow

DOLLY, Edna's dog

EDEN URBANE, a karaoke singing gay terrorist

ESMÉ MASSENGILL, a faded Hollywood vampire

JESUS, Son of God

SPANKY BISHOP, a vampire actor

UTA HÄAGEN-DAZ, a silent screen star vampire

FLUFFER, the stage manager

DON DIVINE, a retired veterinarian

OGDEN RAMSAY, Eden's childhood friend

CORA JEAN PICKLES, xylophonist for
The Turnip Corners Ladies' Orchestrale

TIBBY HARBRECHT, town busybody and drummer

WINNIE WISMER, pianist

GRETA DeBOER, guitarist

ARMINA PHILPOTT, clarinetist

THE SETTING
The fictitious town of Turnip Corners, Alberta

THE TIME – the present

Notes on Staging

"Bridge" refers to three modified marionette stage catwalks above the three main acting areas SL, CS and SR. They are three feet above deck level, each being four feet wide. There is a two foot gap between each which Ronnie can straddle to move from one to the other. Most of the marionettes are "long strung", meaning that the strings allow the marionette control to be held from this bridge height, rather than the standard (Theatre of Marionettes) practice of both Ronnie and puppet being on the same deck level. There are only a few short-strung marionettes, specifically the young Esmé figures for the film flashbacks.

"Gallows" indicates a system used to hang a marionette onstage. These are 3/8" steel rods bent into right angles and inserted in pre-drilled holes across the leaning rail, which is slightly lower than Ronnie's waist height when standing on the bridge. This enables him to hang four or five marionettes in one area at a time, either for group scenes, or to leave a character or characters in position while working at another area. "Control" refers to the above-mentioned marionette control to which the strings of the puppet are attached.

The set is primarily exposed steel with a painted wooden floor (deck top) and three decorative panels onstage which are composed of inlaid wood, copper, brass and sheet metal. The panels front the three bridge towers and are three feet high (deck to top of Ronnie's catwalk "floor") and four feet wide. These are the three acting areas, and each represents one of the three main characters (although they are used for various flashbacks and other scenes). SR is Eden Urbane's area, and the panel front features a prominent sheet metal triangle. It has been painted "Pride Pink", although this is distressed and overwashed to cut the colour intensity. CS is Edna Rural's area, and the panel here features an inlay of a sheet metal cross painted "Red Cross Red". SL is Esmé Massengill's area, and here the inlay shows a metal star painted yellow/gold (again distressed and overwashed).

Behind each of these panels are frames which hide special prop puppets such as the oversize "television face" of young Spanky Bishop or Eden on the cross. The SR and SL panels both live in tracks on the edge of their bridge towers and can be raised and locked into position, revealing the settings or figures within. The CS panel lowers, like a drawbridge, and the reverse side of the panel becomes the floor of Edna Rural's house. Edna's wingback chair is attached to the inside panel/"floor" and lowers with the panel each time the drawbridge comes down. When the drawbridge is lowered we are instantly in Edna's living room.

All scenic shifts and changes, such as panels in front of the acting areas on each bridge unit moving up and down, or the band moving in and out, are done manually, either by Ronnie or the stage manager.

The deck is one foot above the stage floor, twenty four feet wide. The acting area is five and a half feet deep. The main area of the deck is wood, painted to resemble (marionette scale) floor planks in stains of oak, sage and browned purple. The tracks for the bandstands echo the look of train tracks running across the width of the acting area. The sides of the deck and the three entrance points are sheet metal. Each bridge tower is two feet deep, with alleys, or entrances, between them. Behind the acting area and bridge towers is an upstage pass-through area with no decking. It is three feet deep to the back wall of steel mesh screening eleven and a half feet high. At the eight foot height is a hanging rail for marionettes, most of which are hung offstage from these. The top of this hanging rail is painted black with highway lanes for the final image in the show. The back of each bridge tower also has hanging rails for the main characters and their duplicates (e.g.: most of the Esmé puppets are hung on the back of the SL bridge tower). The top three and a half feet of the back wall has a mural of a grain elevator/prairie horizon in the same materials of wood, copper, sheet metal, brass and steel mesh screening, all of which is rusted and overwashed to cut intensity.

Props and furniture either live under each bridge tower or on the two side bridges (which are additional to the main three acting bridges). These side bridges are two feet wide and five feet deep and serve as both structural bracing for the deck and back wall, as well as points for the SM to climb up and down from the upstage passage. Since all puppets and props are contained within the framework of the set, there is no need for any offstage activity or storage during the performance.

The play is performed solely by Ronnie Burkett, and reference to him is throughout the staging directions. The stage manager Terri Gillis is onstage throughout the play, calling sound and lighting cues from a wireless headset, as well as doing pre-sets of scenes and passing marionettes to and from Ronnie. Standard staging abbreviations are used in this text, USC meaning "upstage centre", SL meaning "stage left", "SM" referring to the stage manager and so on.

When a number appears after a character name in the stage directions, such as "Edna #3", it indicates a character represented by duplicate marionettes. This is most usually for costume changes, which require a separate figure for each. Esmé Massengill, for example, is represented at three different ages and numerous costume changes by eleven different marionettes.

Cathy Nosaty's score and sound design and Bill Williams' lighting design are integral to the overall design and performance, although sound and lighting notes within this text are referred to only when necessary to the reading.

The play is performed without intermission, with a running time of approximately 2:12.

Street of Blood premièred at Manitoba
Theatre Centre/Winnipeg in April 1998.
Subsequent runs include The National Arts Centre/Ottawa,
One Yellow Rabbit, The Secret Theatre/Calgary,
Theatre Network/Edmonton, Canadian Stage Company/Toronto,
New York Theater Workshop and the
Henson International Festival of Puppetry/New York City,
Södra Teatern/Stockholm, The Brighton Festival/England,
queerupnorth & Library Theatre/Manchester,
Production retired June 2002 at The Tramway/Glasgow, Scotland.

Produced by Rink-A-Dink Inc./Ronnie Burkett Theatre of Marionettes

Music and Sound Design by ***Cathy Nosaty***

Lighting Design by ***Bill Williams***

Stage Managed by ***Terri Gillis***

Marionettes, Costumes and Set Designed by ***Ronnie Burkett***

Set built by ***Martin Herbert***

Costumes and quilts built by ***Kim Crossley***

Marionettes built by ***Ronnie Burkett***

Studio assistant and additional sculpting, ***Angela Talbot***

Marionette controls, ***Luman Coad***

Puppet Workshop assistants, ***Larry Smith*** *and* ***Charleen Wilson***

Welding by ***Wendy Hogan***

Decorative metal work by ***Jeff DeBoer*** *&*
The Little Giant Rocket Company

Scenic Painter, ***Linda Leon***

Music Recording produced by ***Mark Korven***

for

Eileen & Ray Burkett

At the five minute call, Ronnie and the SM walk onstage and climb onto the bridge. House lights remain up in their preset level. As the audience continues to enter the theatre, Ronnie walks each member of the band—"The Turnip Corners Ladies' Orchestrale"—onstage. Each of the Orchestrale members enter separately and "tune up", the disjointed musical sounds pre-recorded as separate tracks.

The bandstand is actually two separate areas, SR and SL. These are two small wagons, which can move across stage to be joined, or which can slide independently. SL houses the piano and the xylophone, and SR holds the other three instruments and players.

The Orchestrale is composed of five elderly women, all dressed in faded finery. First to enter is Winnie Wismer. She walks onstage from the alley between the SR bridge and side tower, shuffles to centre where she addresses the audience.

WINNIE: Ladies and Gentlemen, the performance will begin in five minutes. There's no intermission, dears, so if you have to piddle, please go now. Thank you.

She turns and shuffles toward the SL band area. She sits on the bench, assisted by the SM and plunks out a few notes. Winnie's control is hung from a gallows rod attached to the bandstand (not the bridge) and left seated at the piano.

Next in is Greta DeBoer, who enters from SL carrying her guitar. She makes her way to the SR bandstand, tunes up and is hung from a gallows.

Miss Armina Philpott enters with her clarinet from the alley between the CS and SR bridges. She is also walked to the SR bandstand where she warms up and is suspended.

Mrs. Tibby Harbrecht enters from the alley between the SR bridge and side tower and makes her way to the drums SR. She sits behind them and has a go.

The last member of the band to enter (from the alley between the SR bridge and side tower) is Cora Jean Pickles. She walks to the SL bandstand.

Once Cora Jean has reached the xylophone, it is Curtain. House lights and pre-set fade slowly as a special on Winnie at the piano, SL band area, crossfades up. She begins to play a short piano "overture" version of "Behold, The Blessed Prairie".

Edna #1 walks onstage and addresses the audience, standing in front of her panel CS.

EDNA: Hello, and welcome to Turnip Corners, Alberta. I'm Edna. Edna Rural. Mrs. Stanley Rural. Now, I'm not an actress. Lord love a duck no! I'm no-one special. I'm just a silly old biddy in a Sears housedress, just like you.

The SL bandstand tracks in to CSL.

WINNIE: Edna!

EDNA: Oh, hello, Winnie dear! That's Winnie Wismer, our pianist.

WINNIE: Edna! What are you doing?

EDNA: Nothing. I'm starting.

WINNIE: Aren't you forgetting something?

EDNA: No. Probably. Yes. What?

WINNIE: Them.

She looks to the audience.

EDNA: No, I've been talking to them, dear.

WINNIE: I mean them and us.

EDNA: Oh yes, of course. That. My apologies. When you're ready, Winnie.

WINNIE: Thank you, Edna. We're ready.

The bandstands track into position CS during Edna's following:

EDNA: Ladies and Gentlemen, please rise for our national anthem, as played by The Turnip Corners Ladies' Orchestrale. Now I'm not kidding, dears. Stand up. Come on. Pretend you're at a hockey game. We're not going any further until we get this over with. This wouldn't be a problem if we were in the United States of America. They might be a war-hungry bunch of bullies, but at least they're patriotic. Now please, stand up! All right, ladies, you may begin.

The ladies begin a spirited, if somewhat awful, version of "O! Canada". The audience is encouraged—or bullied, if need be—to sing along. At the conclusion, the bandstand splits and returns to far SR and SL.

Thank you, dears. You may be seated. Well, let's not stand out here. Come on inside.

Edna's CS panel is lowered, revealing her living room. She sits in her chair. SM places the dog Dolly on the floor by Edna.

There, that's better. And you have my every assurance that "O! Canada" will stand as the sole bit of audience participation for the evening. There will be no singing of "God Save the Queen" at show's end. Lord love a duck no! I'm off the Royal Family. A bunch of inbred yahoos who can't keep their knickers on straight, if you ask my opinion. Now I don't blame the Queen. It's hard for a woman to have a full-time job and raise a family, especially when you're married to a lay-about la-de-da like Philip, so it's not her fault that she's raised a horsey girl, a fat boy, a fruitcake and a fairy. Lord love a duck, that's enough to make anyone a sourpuss with a purse. They had a chance in Diana, and look how they messed that up. Poor Princess Di. I loved that little gal. She took all my risks for me. Too bad the Queen had her murdered in Paris. But none us, not even the Queen herself, ever know the saints when they're amongst us, do we?

Listen to me! Lord love a duck, I barely know you and I'm talking your ears off. Who am I to talk about Her Majesty the Queen of England?! Who gives a tiddly-boo what I think? I'm just a silly old biddy in a Sears housedress, that's who.

She looks at the dog on the floor beside her.

Isn't that right, Dolly? Poor Dolly, my little Crazydoll. You're not doing too well, are you dear? Pretty soon it'll be time for Saint Diana to gather you into her angel arms and take you to your reward too.

The SM enters and places a section of quilting into Edna's hands.

Thank you, dear.

SM exits.

Local girl, comes in to help out every now and then. We grow 'em big around here! Although, I don't think her marriage prospects are very good. She's been running with a queer crowd lately. Anyways, where was I? Oh yes, speaking of the great beyond, you know what my idea of Heaven is? Heaven is a place where you don't worry about money. Ever. Funny how important we make it down here though. I can't honestly remember a day in my adult life when I haven't worried about money. Did I have enough? If I bought this or that, would it throw us off the precarious balance known as getting by and into the pit of eternal debt? Every time I bought myself something, like this dress for instance, it became a question as to whether or not I was worth spending money on. That's been my whole life.

Oh I know what you're thinking. How on earth does this silly old biddy in a Sears housedress know she's going to Heaven? Well my dears, there's no guarantee whatsoever that I will see the Pearly Gates. But I've fed my family three meals a day all these years on a strict budget. I've done more exotic things with macaroni than most women would ever even dream of. And I've worried about money for fifty-one years of my married life. Lord love a duck, that's got to count for something, I'm sure of it. And if there's one thing I am, it's positive.

Light level on her area fades out. Music transition in. Lights come up SR as Ronnie places Eden #1 in front of his panel. The lighting is very dream-like. Suspended around him are clear spheres, each containing a fetus/baby.

EDEN: I've been dreaming of this. I've been dreaming of babies. Really. All these babies, floating. And I'm with them. Not one of them, but there. Seeing things from their point of view. We're floating...inside. Something. Somewhere. And it's always the same. Whenever we start coming out, it ends. A flash of light too bright, walls of skin—thighs, I think—and then... And then I can't remember anything. Just that same dream. Over and over.

The baby spheres swing out of the playing area. Light changes to reality.

I got a letter. No return address. No name. Just a note really. Addressed to me, Eden Urbane, care of The Princess of Wales Hospital. I wonder how she even knew to reach me here. Maybe she's been watching me. Maybe she had a private investigator tail me. Cool. How sick and exhilarating to think that she's seen me. That she knows who I am. Well of course she knows me. Well, not really.

Anyway, now it's my turn. My turn to finally see her. My mother. Not my mother that you've just met, not Edna, that's my Mum. My birth mother. The one I've never met. She wants to meet me. All the letter said was, "Turnip Corners. Meet me there. I'm waiting. Your real mother." She wants to meet me. Maybe I'll finally find out what happened after that flash of light. Shit.

Lights out on Eden, and slow fade up on Edna's area CS. Crossing to the centre bridge, Ronnie "knocks" on the metal siding of the tower. This surprises Edna.

EDNA: Oh dear, I've pricked myself!

TIBBY (offstage): Edna, have you heard the news?

EDNA: Just a minute Tibby dear. Oh darn, I'm bleeding.

Tibby enters.

TIBBY: Can't stay long Edna, just thought I'd pop in with the news.

EDNA: Cup of coffee, Tibby?

TIBBY: No time, Edna. Gotta spread the word!

EDNA: What word is that?

TIBBY: Two words, Edna. Esmé Massengill. Esmé Massengill is coming to Turnip Corners! Today! She'll be here today!

EDNA: Esmé Massengill the movie star?

TIBBY: The one and only!

EDNA: Lord love a duck. I thought she was dead.

TIBBY: That's what the tabloids will have you think, but no. She's alive, she's making a comeback and she's making it here!

EDNA: Why on earth would anyone come to Turnip Corners?

TIBBY: She's doing a new musical, and they always work the bugs out in Canada before hitting Broadway.

EDNA: You don't say.

She looks down at her lap.

Oh Lord love a duck! I've bled all over my quilting!

Tibby comes over to Edna, still seated.

TIBBY: It's an interesting design though.

EDNA: It's a special quilt.

TIBBY: No, I mean the blood. It's created quite a picture.

EDNA: Picture?

TIBBY: Yeah, look. It's like...

EDNA: ...a face. Tibby, do you see what I see?

TIBBY: Edna, you're right.

EDNA: It is a face. There's no mistaking it. It's him, Tibby. It's the face of...

TIBBY: Mr. Wayne Newton! Bud and I saw him in Las Vegas two years ago.

EDNA: Not Wayne Newton. Tibby, it's him. It's the Son of God!

TIBBY: Edna, that doesn't look a thing like Elvis.

EDNA: Not Elvis, Tibby! It's Jesus.

Tibby looks again.

TIBBY: Jesus Christ, Edna!

EDNA: Exactly!

TIBBY: Edna, your eyes are strained. That's not Jesus.

EDNA: It is, Tibby. It's him.

She holds up the quilt square.

It's The Shroud of Turnip Corners.

There is a soft hint of the "Techno Jesus" music sting (to come later) as a special comes up on Ronnie's face. For the audience, this will be the "shroud" image. For Edna, the face is still on her quilt square. He talks to Edna.

JESUS: Hello, Edna.

EDNA: Oh don't talk to me, Jesus. Not now. It's too late.

JESUS: Please, Edna. You're bleeding.

EDNA: Go away!

TIBBY: Edna Rural!

EDNA: Not you, Tibby dear, him.

She indicates the quilt square. The special on Ronnie's face fades out.

TIBBY: Edna, everyone knows that Jesus only appears to Catholics, kooks and cripples. You're just a creative bleeder, that's all.

EDNA: Yes, Tibby, of course.

TIBBY: You know, Edna, you really should think about coming on a cruise with me and Bud this winter. They're loads of fun.

EDNA: I'm a prairie girl, Tibby. The only sea I need is those fields out there.

TIBBY: Edna, you sit in this house night and day. We all thought that when...

EDNA: Please, Tibby, don't!

TIBBY: Well Edna, we thought that when you moved into town, you'd use your time to do more things.

EDNA: I do plenty, Tibby. I have my quilt to keep me busy.

TIBBY: You've been working on that quilt for years.

EDNA: It's a big quilt, Tibby!

Tibby starts off, then turns to Edna.

TIBBY: Suit yourself, Edna, but I don't think that's the face of Jesus. He's got more important things to do than have quilting bees with you.

Tibby leaves and is hung backstage. Above Edna, on the bridge, the special comes up again on Ronnie's face.

JESUS: Edna.

EDNA: You're wasting your time, Jesus. You'd be better off appearing to someone else. Someone who...

JESUS: Yes, Edna?

EDNA: Has time for this. For you.

JESUS: Edna...

EDNA: I said not now, thank you very much!

The special on Ronnie's face fades out.

I'd better phone Eden. This is very important. He'll make a pilgrimage home when he hears the news. He's always been Esmé Massengill's biggest fan.

She stands and exits. Lights down on Edna's area, as music transition begins. The drawbridge of the CS panel is raised and lights come up on Eden's area SR. It is still somewhat dream-like, although the baby spheres have been removed.

EDEN: Do you remember that old Esmé Massengill movie from the 1950s called "Pompeii Afternoon"? She played Mamie Idaho, a spinster librarian who found love in the ruins with a penniless count, played by Italian heart-throb Carlo Biscotti. He was one of those barrel-chested foreign daddy types, but I never spent much time looking at him. No way. I was too busy looking at Esmé's clothes! Even playing a spinster from Bumfuck U.S.A. she looked fabulous! Listen to me. I can't believe I just used the word "fabulous". It's so fag hag.

Anyway, there was that scene, y'know the one I mean? Her big acting scene where she was standing up on some mound of rocks or ruins or something, and she extends her hand to the Count...

Music underscoring begins, with seagulls, manipulated on a pole by the SM in front of the CS tower. Ronnie crosses to the CS bridge and walks Young Esmé #1 as Mamie Idaho onto the upper playing area/catwalk. She wears a 50's day ensemble. She "acts" alone to the unseen Count.

ESMÉ/Mamie: Oh Count Calabrese, it's glorious up here. Why you can see everything, and it's all so old! Come see, Count.

COUNT/Male Voice: Mamie, please, let us not be so formal after all we have shared, all we have tasted, all we have explored. Call me...darling.

ESMÉ/Mamie: Yes. Darling! Oh my darling Count, join me here and feast on these splendid ruins.

COUNT/Male Voice: Oh Mamie, I'm coming!

ESMÉ/Mamie: I never knew that life could be so delicious. All I've ever known are the love stories in books back in my lonely library. But I've been so hungry. Hungry for real love with a real man. Be with me now, darling.

COUNT/Male Voice: Yes Mamie, but it's so hard!

ESMÉ/Mamie: Don't struggle so. Let me help. My hand has a firm grip.

EDEN: And then, just as she bent over for the Count, Mamie Idaho lost her footing, and fell...

The Esmé marionette falls to the floor, CS.

ESMÉ/Mamie: Aaaaagghhhhhhhhhhhhhhhhhhhhhh...

She hits the floor and lays dying.

COUNT/Male Voice: Mamie! Darling! Speak to me!

ESMÉ/Mamie: There is nothing for me to say, darling. Our love is forever written in these ruins.

COUNT/Male Voice: Mamie!

ESMÉ/Mamie: *Arrivederci*, baby.

She expires, and is temporarily hung onstage. Ronnie crosses back to the SR bridge to manipulate Eden.

EDEN: And then she died. A Hollywood death. Looking—well there's no other word for it—fabulous!

Light out CS. SM clears the young Esmé/Mamie marionette.

And that's how I feel every time I go onstage. Well, saying I go onstage is a bit of a stretch I know, but it's how I feel when I perform in these places. Hospitals, hospices, nursing homes. Like I'm somehow extending a hand, yet falling. Into their despair. Their sadness. Okay, I know, they don't ask me to sing, and they don't ask me to feel sad for them, but these dying people need me. I think. I know I need them. Because I'm like Mamie Idaho back in her library. Just living my life through the fictions of other people's lives. And the sadder those lives are, the better.

He exits, SR. SFX of "hospital sounds". Dream light crossfades to his "show light". The SM places a mirror ball and a stool onstage. Eden #2 enters from the SL side of the SR tower. He is dressed in a powder blue tuxedo jacket and has a microphone in his hand.

Good afternoon, Ladies and Gentlemen. How's everyone doing today? Obviously not so well or you wouldn't be in a place like this!

"Bad joke" drum sting.

My name is Eden Urbane and I'm the songbird of the sick bay, the crooning chanteur of the ICU, the karaoke king of the cancer ward! I'm here to sing you a few tunes and hopefully bring a little smile to your face. My, what a well dressed crowd we have today! That's a lovely colostomy bag, Mrs. Spudnicki, but trust me hon, you'll never find shoes to match!

Another drum sting.

Thank you! Allow me to introduce the band.

The SM places a boombox on the stool. Eden looks at the mic.

Mind if I call you Mike? With a head like that, you can call me anything!

Drum sting.

Reminds me of a date I had once. But seriously folks, it's my great honour to be in this fine public healthcare facility today with all...(he counts quickly) eleven of you. Ladies and Gentlemen, I would now like to perform for you the love theme from the 1962 horror classic, "House of Pain", in which the incomparable Miss Esmé Massengill played Lotta Payne, a reclusive widow living in a strange hilltop house. Maestro, if you please.

Music intro starts. He sings.

House of Pain

Your love is scaring me to death
I'm speechless
Scaring me to death
And darling
It's cutting off my breath

Your love is making me turn blue
I'm gasping
Making me turn blue
And darling
Strictly *entre nous*
I love this
I'm blue
And scared by love

Yes my heart has become a house of pain
Each room a prison, a torture cell
This sweet paradise is also my hell
I return to again and again
Yes my heart has become a house of pain
I should flee, but why bother trying
Why can't you see, my darling I'm dying
To live in your house of pain

Lights out. Ronnie hangs Eden #2 backstage and crosses to SL bridge. During this, he continues to speak as Eden on the musical playout.

Thank you! What a wonderful crowd. My name is Eden Urbane with Karaoke Memory Lane and I'll be performing for you all afternoon.

Lights up on Esmé's area SL. The panel is not raised. In front of it, posed in tableau, are (L to R) Uta Häagen-Daz, Spanky Bishop #1 and Fluffer, all of whom have been hung from the bridge/gallows by the SM during Eden's patter and song. There are several old-style trunks and suitcases in front of them.

SPANKY: *Oy.* This is some place, this Turnip Corners. I haven't seen a town so small since...well, come to think about it, I've never seen a town this small.

UTA: *Alter wikser* (old jerk off)! *Du bist ein peniskopf* (you're a dickhead)!

FLUFFER: What did she say, Mr. Bishop?

SPANKY: I believe she just called me an old dickhead.

FLUFFER: Oh no oh no oh no, that's terrible, Mr. Bishop!

SPANKY: It's alright, Fluffer. Under the circumstances, I would tend to agree with her.

UTA: *Verfickte hurenscheisse* (over-fucked whore's shit)!

FLUFFER: Mr. Bishop?

SPANKY: Not worth repeating, my dear, not worth repeating. Now, Fluffer my darling, why don't you go see what's holding Miss Massengill up...other than her legs. I love that joke! Get it?

Fluffer laughs, then pauses.

FLUFFER: Um, no, not really, Mr. Bishop.

Fluffer exits in the alley between the SL and CS bridge towers.

SPANKY: *Oy.*

Tibby enters from the alley between the SL and CS bridge towers, handed to Ronnie by the SM. She excitedly makes her way toward Spanky and Uta.

TIBBY: Oh! Thespians! Hello hello hello. Welcome to Turnip Corners! We are so thrilled to have you in our "corner" of the world.

SPANKY: And we are delighted to be in your company, Miss...

TIBBY: Harbrecht. Tibby Harbrecht.

SPANKY: Charmed, Miss Harbrecht.

TIBBY: Actually, it's "Mrs". Mrs. Bud Harbrecht.

SPANKY: Oy, I've been nipped by the Bud!

TIBBY: Oh such talk! You'll turn my head!

SPANKY: Later perhaps. Allow me to introduce myself. Spanky Bishop, at your service.

TIBBY: No! Really? Not the Spanky Bishop?! The Wacky Bellhop himself! I saw every one of your movies... "The Wacky Bellhop in Paris", "The Wacky Bellhop in Love", "The Wacky Bellhop Goes AWOL in Waikiki"...oh, I could go on and on!

SPANKY: No doubt.

UTA: *Schnetzer labarkopf* (loose lipped gossip)! *Arschkricher* (brown nose!)

TIBBY: Oh, and who do we have here? She's such a tiny little thing, I barely noticed her!

SPANKY: This, my dear Mrs. Harbrecht, is the greatest actress ever to grace the silent screen. Miss Uta Häagen-Daz.

UTA: *Pissende dummfotze* (stupid pissing cunt)!

TIBBY: Oh, how European! And "*bidet*" to you too, honey!

Music sting in. Esmé #1 enters and is posed dramatically in the alley between the SL and CS bridge towers. She is fabulous, in a Golden Age of Hollywood kind of way. She is wearing her idea of a travelling/day ensemble. Lots of beads and feathers. In one arm is a vicious white poodle.

ESMÉ: So this is Alberta. Yee haw.

SPANKY: The one, the only, Esmé Massengill!

ESMÉ: Spanky, remind me to kill my agent.

SPANKY: You already did.

TIBBY: I could just lay down and die right here and now!

ESMÉ: What a soothing thought. But darling, the night is young. Let's save the fun for later.

TIBBY: I'm all tongue-tied. My heart's a-racing!

ESMÉ: Oh yummy.

TIBBY: We are so honoured to have you in our fair town Miss Massengill.

ESMÉ: Thank You. We're glad to be...anywhere.

SPANKY: You know the tour's bad when you look forward to Regina.

Esmé's poodle barks and snarls at Tibby.

TIBBY: What an adorable dog. Hello sweetie.

ESMÉ: Please don't touch her. She's an absolute bitch.

TIBBY: What's her name?

ESMÉ: Dorothy Barker. She plays a lamb in my new show.

TIBBY: And what is your new musical about, if I may be so bold?

ESMÉ: It's called "Oh Mary!". The life of the Virgin Mary, told in word and song and dance. I of course portray the titular role of Mary, the Virgin. Mr. Bishop here is Joseph.

TIBBY: And Miss Häagen-Daz?

ESMÉ: The angel who appears to Joseph, telling him to take flight to Egypt. It's a dance role.

TIBBY: And the wise men?

ESMÉ: There are no wise men. Especially not in the theatre. No, we're going rather minimalist on this one. Bare bones, pared down and bold in its simplicity.

SPANKY: Our backer died.

ESMÉ: So sue me, I like a nosh. *Et voilà!* We find ourselves here. Extraordinary talent, a few simple costumes, but no scenery, and alas, no band. A musical without musicians!

TIBBY: Oh, but that's not a problem! I'm with The Turnip Corners Ladies' Orchestrale. We'd be honoured to play for your show!

ESMÉ: Fortune smiles upon us! Lovely. I'll have my stage manager Fluffer arrange the rehearsal details with you.

TIBBY: Well, you must be exhausted after your trip.

ESMÉ: Not really, we sleep all day.

TIBBY: How bohemian!

ESMÉ: Technically it's Romanian, but why quibble.

UTA: *Spermaschlucker* (sperm swallower)!

ESMÉ: That's enough Uta! Spanky, be a darling and escort Miss Häagen-Daz to her dressing room.

SPANKY: Certainly.

Spanky and Uta exit.

ESMÉ: And Spanky, keep an eye on her. You know how our Uta gets when she's hungry.

She turns to Tibby.

Speaking of which, any thoughts on where I could get a bite?

TIBBY: How about a nice big steak!

Esmé shudders.

ESMÉ: No stake!

TIBBY: Well, there's The Red Lantern Café, home of Chinese and Canadian cuisine. Bit of everything on the menu, but I'm sure you'll find something to satisfy you.

ESMÉ: I think I already have. My tastes are so simple.

TIBBY: Lovely! Well then, follow me.

Tibby leaves and is handed to the SM.

ESMÉ: I'm right behind you. Come, Dorothy darling, dinner is served! Mummy will save you a bone!

Esmé exits. SM clears the luggage. Lights SL out. As soon as they begin to dim, we hear SFX of Edna (pre-recorded) on Eden's answering service. This message plays over the transition as the SM lowers the drawbridge panel into Edna's living room and places Dolly #2 on the chair.

EDEN (recorded): Hi, you've reached the voicemail for Eden Urbane and his Karaoke Memory Lane. Please leave your message after the tone and I'll call

you back as soon as I can. And remember, follow the bouncing balls! *Ciao!*

EDNA (recorded): Eden? Edie dear, are you there? Can you hear me? Pick up. Eden, it's me. Pick up. It's Mum. Edie, pick up if you can hear me. Are you listening? (pause) Well, I guess you're not there. Are you there? I guess not. Anyways, just thought I'd call to see how you're doing. I'm fine, not much going on. Crazydoll's gonna die soon, Esmé Massengill is in town, and Jesus Christ has appeared to me on a quilt square. No need to call back. Just thought I'd say hi. Okay then, bye bye.

SFX of the end of the phone call. Lights up CS. Edna #2 is dressed in her nightie and robe, and is standing SL of her chair, looking down at Dolly. Standing SR of the chair is Don Divine. He is a rather dashing older man.

EDNA: So that's it then, eh?

DON: I'm sorry Edna. These dogs get to a certain age and there's not much we can do for them.

EDNA: I just hate to see her suffer.

DON: Oh, she's having a bit of a time breathing, but I don't think she's in pain. You're just slowing down, aren't you Dolly?

EDNA: Do you think we should...you know...help her off to sleep?

DON: I think she'll just drift off when it's her time. But if she takes a turn for the worse Edna, you call Dr. Talbot and he'll make the end easier for you both. Or give me a call and I'll drive the old girl over to him for you.

EDNA: Oh, you've already done more than enough, Dr. Divine.

DON: Please Edna, it's Don. I'm not a practicing veterinarian anymore. And I was hoping you'd start thinking of me as something else.

EDNA: Oh?

DON: A friend. A neighbour. We're both townies now, so we gotta stick together eh?

Edna becomes a bit uncomfortable, embarrassed.

EDNA: Lord love a duck! Look at me standing here in my nightie. Practically nude! You must think I'm a terrible old hussy.

DON: Not at all. Perfectly natural to be in your pajamas at this hour.

EDNA: And me calling you over here in the middle of the night! I'm just a silly old biddy I am. It's just that I was so worried about Dolly and I didn't know what else to do.

DON: You did the right thing, Edna.

There's an awkward pause as they lean into one another over the chair.

Well, I'll let you get some sleep.

EDNA: Let me pay you for your trouble.

DON: Wouldn't hear of it, dear lady.

EDNA: Well that's awfully kind of you...Don.

DON: But there is something I would like, Edna.

She retreats a bit.

EDNA: Oh?

DON: There's a dinner and dance for the Prairie Revival Party next week. Oh, these political things can be a bit long-winded, but it's for a good cause. And I would be honoured if you'd attend, as my guest.

EDNA: Your guest?

DON: My date.

EDNA: Your date.

DON: Yes.

EDNA: Don Divine! What in Sam Hill do you think I am? Some free love floozy you can romance like a cheap dame in the movies?

DON: No, of course not. Edna, please, you misunderstand.

EDNA: No Don, you misunderstand. I'm a married woman.

DON: I'm sorry Edna. I've been so lonely since my Dora died.

I guess I thought you'd be interested in some company too.

EDNA: Company is all fine and well Don. But dinner and dancing and dates, well, that's just taking it a bit too far. Stanley Rural is the only man I've ever been with, and I intend to keep the vows of my marriage intact.

DON: But Edna, we have to move on.

EDNA: I am a married woman...Doctor Divine. I will always be a married woman. Now, if you'll excuse me, I have my quilt to finish. Good night.

DON: Good night, Edna.

He leaves. Edna stares after him momentarily, then turns with a sigh.

EDNA: I guess I'll make myself a Neo Citran. It's the only thing that gets me to sleep these days. Warm milk just gives me gas, and hot toddies make me tipsy. No, a nice hot

Neo is the only thing that knocks me out. Sometimes I have a double, but only if I've watched the CBC News and upset myself.

She exits CSR as light fades out. The SM strikes Dolly and raises the drawbridge of Edna's panel. Small spot on Eden #1, SR.

EDEN: I once knew a male nurse whose cock was so big, every time he got an erection he would faint. Imagine that. A boner so big it drains the blood right out of your brain. Now that's passion!

For six years I lived with the nicest man. Anthony. Eden and Anthony. We were the perfect couple. Everyone told us so. I was in love. Once. A long time ago. But it was brutal. It wasn't Anthony, although I grew to be afraid of him too.

See, Anthony looked like a gay icon. Like those perfect, ridiculous, empty men in underwear ads. V-shaped, hairless, air-brushed. And that's really fucking hard to be around, man, because it caused me to look at myself a considerable amount more than I prefer. Who can look that much sadness and anger in the face? Not me. Not when when it's mine. But we had everything. Except passion. And besides, I couldn't leave him. We had too much stuff.

One Saturday afternoon I was lying on the couch while Anthony was in the basement working out. And there on TV was my sign—my epiphany—in the form of an old Esmé Massengill movie, "No Room For Love", in which she played Constance Hart, a wealthy society dame married to an abusive banker who forfeits comfort and home and social standing to run off with a long-haul trucker named Butch, played brilliantly by Armand Collier. Butch. Oh hump-daddy Butch. That guy was as dangerous as day-old sushi.

Light dims somewhat on Eden as it comes up on young Esmé #2, atop the SR catwalk, posed in a spectacular gown. Esmé "acts" alone to an unseen male voice. The flashback is underscored with lush, overly-romantic movie music.

ESMÉ/Constance: I love you Hy, and I've tried to make you love me. But you've left me, and left me with no choice.

HY/Male Voice: I've never left you Constance. I'm here! Right here, just as I've always been.

ESMÉ/Constance: No, you're distant Hy. You've gone far, far away, to a land where love cannot live.

HY/Male Voice: I've given you everything a woman could ever want, Connie. Money, clothes, jewels. That's love, isn't it?

ESMÉ/Constance: No, Hy! We've crowded our lives with things, and left no room for the most important thing of all. We've left no room for love!

The movie music swells dramatically as Esmé hits her final pose and exits. Lights fade on the flashback area and restores on Eden.

EDEN: Once again, Esmé came through for me! She was my inspiration. Fuck the house. Screw the stuff. Okay, so I didn't have a long-haul trucker waiting for me, but I had a car. A 1986 powder blue Monte Carlo. I got up off that couch and packed. Favorite clothes, photo albums, some books, my pipe bomb stuff, the duvet and two pillows, all the CDs that were mine, a boom box, and almost anything that was battery operated. And the cell phone. I was on the run, true, but I still needed access to my voicemail. Into the car it went. I had found my new home. And my escape. It was decided and done, start to finish, in thirty-five minutes.

Thirty-five minutes. It took six years to build something, to accumulate all the trappings, and thirty-five minutes to end it. But then, destruction is always quicker than creation. And way more noticeable.

I went downstairs to tell Anthony I was leaving. "Keep the house, keep everything, I have to go. I can't stay here anymore. I can't stay with you". And he started to cry. Well, I like to think they were tears, not just sweat running down his face. Eventually he spoke. "It's because I bore you, isn't it?"

Of course I lied. I said no.

And left. But lemme tell ya, life isn't like the movies. In "No Room For Love", just as Constance and Butch finally hit the road, they both die when the truck skids off a bridge in the rain. My fate was worse. I lived.

In my car. Really. I am one of the intentionally homeless. It's okay, and once you figure out which bathrooms to use it becomes easier. "No fixed address", that's me. Kind of implies I'm going somewhere, doesn't it? I guess you could say I'm presently between lifestyles. But hey, what fag isn't?

Anyway, I'm going home. Not to Anthony. To Turnip Corners. To visit my Mum. And to meet my mother. My real mother. Esmé! Oh shit, I'm afraid again. Maybe I should blow something up before I hit the road. That always makes me feel better. Nah, I'd miss all the press coverage.

Lights out on Eden, who exits via the alley right of the SR bridge. Music in for the "Techno Jesus" sound and light show. This segment is loud, chaotic, intense, modern. Ronnie crosses to the SL bridge tower, places Esmé #2 on her chaise, and as the transition ends there is a blast of smoke from under the catwalk. Ronnie ends on the SL leaning rail, arms outstretched. Light up on Esmé and a special on Ronnie's face above.

ESMÉ: Now that's an entrance!

JESUS: Miss Massengill. We need to talk.

ESMÉ: Well, if it isn't the Only Begotten. Iesus Nazarenus Rex Iudaeorum.

JESUS: Very good Esmé! I never would have guessed you to know Latin.

ESMÉ: Pish, darling, it's the perfect language for me. Dead.

JESUS: Well, you are starting to look your age, Esmé.

ESMÉ: And you've put on weight, bitch, but did I bring that up?

JESUS: Look, I'm not here to fight.

ESMÉ: Then what brings you here? Surely the good folk of Turnip Corners aren't so important that they warrant an appearance by you.

JESUS: There's two I thought I should keep an eye on.

ESMÉ: To protect them from me? Aren't you sweet!

JESUS: To protect them from themselves.

ESMÉ: Darling, you've been off the circuit for so long people wouldn't recognize you if they saw you. But have you seen what your competition's been up to lately?

JESUS: I keep tabs on him.

ESMÉ: Cable, multinationals, the Moral Majority, all of Hollywood, and of course, Satan's craftiest minion on earth, the Internet. It's gorgeous, and so simple.

JESUS: Don't be fooled by the appearance of simplicity Esmé.

ESMÉ: But it is simple darling, and he's the one who figured it out, not you. Give them sex, everywhere! Let them diddle themselves in front of a computer screen, with a video or on their cellular phones. Swell their loins and drain the blood out of their brains. Let the new millennium sneak up and catch them all with their pants down!

JESUS: Alright Esmé, enough. Why are you here?

ESMÉ: Oh, I'm doing out-of-town try outs with my new show.

JESUS: Esmé, it's me.

ESMÉ: Well darling, being here is part of the plan. Actually, it is the plan.

JESUS: What plan?

ESMÉ: It's blood darling. Pure, uncontaminated blood. Oh not for me. I'll drink any plasma you put in front of me. But for stockpiling, for hoarding, for selling, well, for that, I need the quality stuff.

JESUS: Selling?

ESMÉ: Yes. Because he—or rather, she—who controls the blood supply controls the world. You can blood bank on it. And besides, feeding on victim after victim got a bit tedious after awhile. So now we still have the thrill of seduction and attack, make the puncture, have a little sip and drain the rest for storage. And the product tends to be purer in the sticks.

JESUS: Esmé, promise me you'll leave my two people alone.

ESMÉ: We'll see darling, we'll see.

JESUS: You may have a fight on your hands this time, Esmé.

ESMÉ: Delicious! So you think you're finally up to me?

JESUS: What makes you think I was talking about me?

Light out on Ronnie and Esmé SL. Short "Techno Jesus" sting, dissolving into theme for Edna. Slow crossfade up on CS. The SM strikes the chaise and lowers the drawbridge panel. Ronnie hangs Esmé backstage, crosses to CS bridge tower and walks Edna #2 into the scene.

EDNA: I've been awake all night. Two Neo Citrans and I still couldn't sleep. Maybe it was the late show that did it. They were showing that old Esmé Massengill movie, "Passport to Love". It was one of my favorites. Esmé played Dixie Carlyle, a waitress in a roadside diner who changes a flat tire for a travelling foreign prince and falls in love. Oh, so romantic. But that was our Esmé. Living, breathing passion!

Light dims somewhat CS. Ronnie leaves Edna sitting in her chair and crosses to the SL bridge tower, walking Young Esmé #3 onto the catwalk. This is a contained pool of light, revealing Esmé in a spectacular white satin wedding dress with a pale pink beaded veil. Again, Esmé stands alone and the people to whom she is speaking are unseen. This is heavily underscored with movie music.

ESMÉ/Dixie: Oh Betty, oh Audrey, oh Delores, why you're the best friends a gal could ever have. Thanks for coming all the way to this foreign country just to be my bridesmaids. I'll miss you all and the happy times we had at the diner. Oh sure, here they'll call me Princess, but I'll always be Diner Dixie to you. Please know that I will never forget you gals, nor will I ever forget that it was slinging hash that brought me to the palace gates. But now I say goodbye, my beloved Ladies in Waitressing, for my heart has a new destination and my passport is love! Prince darling, wait for me!

She turns upstage as the music swells. SFX of honking car horn and screeching tires as SL light to black. Young Esmé is hung backstage, Ronnie crosses to CS bridge and Edna's light restores.

EDNA: Too bad poor Dixie Carlyle tripped on the train of her dress and got hit by a speeding taxi as she crossed the street to the church. But she died beautifully, and oh, I loved that dress! More than anything I had ever

seen. So when my Stanley asked me to help run the farm—which was his idea of a marriage proposal—I just knew that my wedding dress had to be like the one in "Passport to Love".

I saw that movie three times down at the old Bijoux, trying to doodle the dress in the dark. I clipped every picture I could find of it from the movie magazines. I worked extra hours at Turner's Drugstore during the week, just so I could save enough money to buy five yards of satin and two of lace from the catalogue, shipped all the way from Toronto.

I made my pattern from old newspapers, then I cut it out of sugar sacks, like I use for my quilting, as a kind of test run. Then I scrubbed down the kitchen table, laid out my precious cloth, and cut. Lord love a duck, I had never been so nervous in my whole life. It took me weeks to sew that dress, because I knew that fancy clothes in France were all hand sewn. And since necessity is the mother of invention, I stained the lace veil pink by dipping it in a bucket of diluted saskatoons I'd put through the sieve.

Leaving Edna seated in her chair CS, Ronnie crosses to SL bridge.

I knew I was no Esmé Massengill, and even though I stopped eating the week before the wedding, I was still just lumpy Edna. But when I put on that dress, well, didn't I just feel like a princess.

Young Edna #1 enters through the alley between the SL and CS bridges. She is in her wedding dress, a copy of the one from Esmé's movie. She walks SLC to a phrase of "Here Comes The Bride", and is hung in position there.

It was a small wedding and I had only one gal stand up with me, not a tribe of bridesmaids like Esmé. There was no money for that, and besides, I didn't have that many friends.

Light up on Cora Jean at the SL bandstand.

But Cora Jean Pickles, who worked with me at the drugstore, agreed to be my bridesmaid and matron of honour combined. Cora Jean was saving up her money to go to Winnipeg to study the ballet. It was Cora Jean who gave me the beads for my veil. Took them right off one of her dance recital dresses. I was indebted to her for life because of that.

Light fades out on Cora. Ronnie crosses back to the CS bridge and Edna.

I don't remember much about my wedding day. Oh I know it's supposed to be the most important day in a woman's life, but I had worked and worried so much on an empty stomach that I was in kind of a fog. Mind you, the fog lifted that night when Stanley...took his husbandly way with me. Suddenly I didn't feel like a princess anymore. So, the next morning I wrapped that dress in tissue paper and put it away in the cedar chest.

Light SL dims on young Edna, but not to black.

And we got on with our married life, which was surprisingly not much different from life before. I even grew to tolerate Stanley climbing on top of me at night, sometimes imagining that he was Armand Collier or Trevor St. Clair or some other movie star lover. Looking back I realise now that it never really took that long anyway, although it seemed like an eternity at the time. But it was my duty, and it would hopefully lead to something.

But it never did. After awhile, I went to old Doctor Beaton to see if I was doing something wrong. But no, he assured me that we were doing everything right. It was my body that was wrong. It could not, it would not make a baby. They used to call it barren. Like the prairie when the fields are empty. That was me. Empty, through and through.

When I got home, Stanley was still out doing the chores. To this day I don't know why, but I went to the cedar chest, took out my wedding dress and put it on. And went upstairs and sat on the bed. It was the only night in my married life when I didn't make supper.

Light up, just barely, on young Edna SL. SM hands Ronnie a black cap, which he puts on as Stanley.

Stanley found me sitting there. He didn't say a word. Not a peep. Stood in the doorway staring at me. I couldn't look at him, but I told him. "I can't have a baby" was all I said. Stanley was so quiet. He left the room. I stayed on the bed, memorising the rag rug on the floor, listening to him downstairs. A terrible racket. I thought he was breaking things, or packing to leave. I didn't know.

Light intensity shifts somewhat in a subtle crossfade from Edna in chair CS to young Edna SL. CS does not fade to black. Continuing Edna's storytelling, Ronnie leaves the CS marionette, walks toward SL and climbs off the bridge to deck level. He is Stanley. During the following monologue, Ronnie enacts what Edna is describing. The bacon and eggs are mimed, but the apron is real, and he ties it onto the marionette during the description.

And then he was there again. He set something down on the bureau, walked over to me and tied an apron around me while I sat. Then he took what he had set on the bureau and put it on my lap. I looked down and there was a plate. Bacon and eggs. He knelt down, took a piece of bacon in his fingers, and held it up to my mouth. That's when we looked at each other. We stayed there for a long, long time. Me in my wedding dress and an apron, Stanley on his knees before me. Me and my man. Mr. and Mrs. Stanley Rural. Crying over a plate of bacon and eggs.

He ends on his knees, embracing young Edna. The tableau of Ronnie and young Edna in her wedding dress is held as the SL light fades very slowly to black. Ronnie strikes young Edna #1 and resumes his place on the bridge, SL. Lights up on Eden's area SR as Ronnie crosses from SL bridge to SR.

EDEN: Do you ever think about those people you called fag in school? No, of course you don't. But we think about you. All the time. Imagine that in every town all over the world there were a few of those kids. Nice kids, whose only hope of survival was to get out. And man, I got out. To the city.

In the city you have access to...more. More activity, more noise, more movies, more shopping, more people, more stuff, more sex. Oh yeah, I had a lot of sex when I first got there. A lot. I suppose I'm kind of your worst nightmare. A fag who has had as much sex as you think fags have.

Lights crossfade. Down a bit on Eden (who is hung from the gallows and remains in position SR), and up on Edna in her chair CS.

EDNA: It was Thanksgiving, 1982. Eden had already been living in the city for several years, ever since he graduated from high school. Like a bullet from a pistol, that's how he got out of this town. So every now and then, I'd pack my plaid overnight case and take the bus into the city to see him. The train had stopped coming through Turnip Corners years ago, even though we clung to these tracks and the grain elevator as some sort of memento of when the town had had a soul. Same reason I'd go see my Edie. To remind myself that we were a family still.

Now, Mr. Stanley Rural did not join me on these Greyhound adventures. Never cared much for the bus. Certainly did not care for the city. And although it was never discussed, I felt that something had stopped him from caring about Eden too.

Anyways, a week before Thanksgiving 1982, Eden phoned to say that he was coming home. And bringing a couple of friends. Well, Lord love a duck, didn't that just throw me into a tizzy! Why, there were mattresses to turn, beds to make up, pies and jellied salads to get prepared, the good china to get out and wash up. And I needed Stanley to drive me into the IGA so I could get the biggest turkey they had. Oh, but I didn't mind all the fuss and bother. This was one Thanksgiving I had something to be thankful for. My Eden was coming home.

Lights crossfade again. Up on Eden SR.

EDEN: I learned how to make bombs on the Internet. Nothing fancy, just pipe bombs and fire explosives. Simple stuff. I could have gotten more elaborate I suppose, but I hated surfing through all those militia pages. Hundreds and hundreds of websites devoted to my extinction. Man, I had no idea I was such a threat to them. Cool.

My first bomb was actually intended for a Prairie Revival Party campaign rally. See, they were making all this Christian bullshit noise about "the homosexual agenda". Man, someone should have told them you can't organise fags to agree on anything. But just when we thought it was safe to poke our heads out of the trenches and wave our little rainbow flags, the enemy pounced. And man, those fuckers are organised. And all the gay activists could do was to mount a lame campaign to prove how normal we are. Fuck that. What needed to happen was to prove how dangerous those people are to me. I mean, to us. Look, I'm no activist, okay? I don't ask for my right to be. I'm a radical. I take it.

So I changed my plan and set my first pipe bomb off in the back entrance of Tongue in Cheek, one of the more popular gay bars. It was a Monday night, so there were only a handful of patrons, and I knew they were all in the front bar. The blast didn't cause any injuries, and not a lot of damage. But the effect was fucking enormous. A gay bar had been bombed. The cops took it seriously, the press covered it, and best of all, the gay community got scared. Really scared. Junior high scared. And indirectly, fingers started pointing at the Prairie Revival Party. Jackpot!

So that weekend I set off another one at a lesbian coffee shop called Sappho's Grind. I felt kinda bad, 'cause it was a nice place. But I had to involve the dykes too. I mean, think about it. They're gay and female, so there's double the oppression. Which means double the rage. And rage is what I'm interested in.

Tick tick tick tick...kaboom, baby.

Lights crossfade. Up on Edna, CS.

EDNA: Eden's friends were, now let me see...there was a pale, skinny boy named Kiki, and a largish girl named Jane spelled d-j-a-n-e with the "d" being silent. They didn't say much to me, and most of what they said to Edie was whispered. Djane sat in the kitchen a few times, not to lift a finger and help out, but to lecture me on how degrading my role as a homemaker was to my "woman spirit". She did manage to eat most of the baking I'd put out, although I don't think she realised that this was a direct result of my chosen profession. And she felt that my saying "Lord love a duck" gave too much power to an unseen male force with a controlling agenda. Better, she thought, to say "Goddess love all the ducks, big and small, of all colours and gender persuasions". What a cornflake!

Stanley had found all sorts of work to do out in the quonset shed. Barely showed his face around the house the whole time we had Edie and his friends. But this was a holiday dinner—a prairie woman's showcase—and I marched myself out to that shed and told Mr. Stanley Rural to wash up, suit up and show up at my table on time or there would be hell to pay. I put up with a lot, but don't mess with me when there's a turkey involved!

Lights crossfade. Up on Eden, SR.

EDEN: I knew what my third target would have to be. There's a small alternative high school, and they had a program for gay kids. Kids who had really suffered in the mainstream system. And it was something the community had fought and worked for a long time, because, well, let's face it man, we all remembered high school.

Ronnie pauses, looks straight out to the audience and remembers.

RONNIE: Fucking high school.

EDEN: Anyway, it was the only bomb that I ever had second thoughts about, but I knew its impact would be the last straw. It had to be done. So late one night I broke in, set up and blew the shit out of that school. And I can't tell you how fucking good that felt. And this time, I left a calling card. Out on the sidewalk I spray painted two pink words. Purse Boy. That's all it said.

Lights up on Edna, CS.

EDNA: Thanksgiving dinner. There we sat, the five of us. Or rather, me and the silent quartet. Now you may have noticed, I tend to go on a bit. And when I'm nervous, well my chin wagging just won't stop. So I talked. I passed the turkey, and I talked. I passed the dressing, and I talked. I passed the gravy boat, and talked. I passed the potatoes, the turnips, the peas and the corn and I talked and talked and talked and talked. I was just about to pass around the jellied salad—oh, the clear green one with fruit cocktail in it, not the creamy ambrosia one with the Philadelphia cream cheese and pineapple tidbits—when Eden stood up, cleared his throat and said:

EDEN: Mum. Dad. I'm gay.

EDNA: I didn't know what to do. I'd planned this for a week, and now it had all gone wrong. Maybe there wasn't enough food. I held the jellied salad in front of Djane and said "This one has fruit in it".

EDEN: Mum! Didn't you hear me? I said I'm gay. Don't you have anything to say about that?

EDNA: Well, for once I was silent. It was dead quiet at that table. That eerie kind of stillness like right before a big storm. And I could feel him. From the other end of that table, my Stanley, starting to vibrate like a generator getting going. All in his neck, eh? His neck doubling in size and ready to burst. And his face. Eyes crazy like an animal, ready to attack. And getting all red, like every drop of blood in his body had rushed to his head. This had gone terribly wrong. This was all my fault. I should have cooked a ham too!

Suddenly, Stanley slammed his cutlery down on his plate with a crash. Put both hands on the table and lifted himself up to his full height. He looked bigger than I'd ever seen him before. Like a giant. Like a crazy unfriendly giant. And his face was so red it looked like a missile would shoot straight out the top of his head at any moment. I had to do something. Say something. Fix this. Come on Edna, you're a smart woman, you read Chatelaine. Think Edna, think.

Edna stands, half from the excitement of her story-telling, partially as re-enactment.

Dessert. I had dessert! My saviour! I put the jellied salad down, placed my hands on the table and stood opposite Mr. Stanley Rural, staring him down. Oh, not as tall but just as strong-willed. His eyes locked with mine, like two gunfighters, fingers twitching for their pistols. I shot first. I spoke. I spoke as calmly and as bravely and as sensibly as any Canadian woman in my situation would. And I said to him, "Stanley Rural, keep your fork! There's pie."

Edna sits.

He sat down. We finished our meal in silence. I cleared the table. Everyone retained their cutlery. I served dessert. Eden and his friends went back to the city. Stanley went to bed. And I did the dishes, alone. It was an awful Thanksgiving. I didn't even have my slice of the pie.

CS light fades out.

EDEN: My bombs aren't meant to hurt gay people. They're meant to blow the lid off our bottled rage. So watch out, because now there is a homosexual agenda. Fairies are fighting back. And God help anyone who gets in the way of that fury.

Eden's light fades out as he exits R. Music transition, suggesting time change. Ronnie removes Edna #2 and seats Edna #3 in the chair. This is her good dress, not flashy, but from the more expensive part of the Sears ladies wear section. The SM places a box wrapped in Christmas paper DSL of the chair. SFX of a car horn. Lights up CS.

EDNA: Eden, is that you?

Eden #1 enters from the alley between CS and SR bridges.

EDEN : No, it's Gloria Cartier, the orphaned young socialite with amnesia from "Midnight in Monte Carlo"!

EDNA: Oh you! Get in here and give your old mum a hug.

He enters Edna's area, SR of the chair.

EDEN: Hi, Mum.

EDNA: Let me get you something to eat.

EDEN: I'm not hungry, Mum. Sit.

EDNA: You look like a skeleton. How about a grilled cheese?

EDEN: No thanks.

EDNA: I've got some matrimonial cake. Just made it yesterday.

EDEN: Mum, no.

EDNA: Oh, but you always liked my matrimonial cake.

EDEN: Not now, okay?

EDNA: Okay then, I think I've got some Rocky Road Squares with the coloured mini marshmallows in the freezer. Only take a minute to thaw them out...

EDEN: Mum, stop over-functioning.

EDNA: Suit yourself, Mr. Scrawny. How's Tony?

EDEN: Mum, it's Anthony. You never abbreviate a fag's name.

EDNA: Oh. How's Anthony?

EDEN: He's...perfect.

He notices the box on the floor.

Bit early for Christmas.

EDNA: Oh no dear, that's Dolly.

EDEN: What? You wrapped up the dog?

EDNA: She was gathered Edie. Middle of the night, she was taken off to her reward.

EDEN: Mum, this is too weird. Why would you gift wrap a dead dog?

EDNA: Well, you gave her to me as a Christmas present and that's how I'm going to send her off. I've been waiting for you to get here so we could bury her in the backyard. That's why I'm in my fancy dress and wearing my Avon.

EDEN: Poor Crazydoll.

EDNA: I thought you might like to sing that at the service.

EDEN: What?

EDNA: That song. "Crazydoll". From that old Esmé Massengill and Spanky Bishop movie. You used to sing that song at the drop of a hat when you were a kid. Remember?

EDEN: Not really.

EDNA: Sure you do. You'd get up and perform for me, right in front of the television. It was almost like you were on it. Come on Edie, sing a little bit for me.

EDEN: I don't remember it.

EDNA: Well I do. I remember everything. We had just bought the colour TV.

Light CS dims to very low level as we crossfade up SR. The SM has preset a chair like Edna's R of the SR panel. Young Edna #2 is preset in the chair, dressed in a housedress. Beside her is young Eden #1. He is a chubby, pleasant-looking child with the same shock of red hair and glasses. The intro for the song "Crazydoll" plays under the initial dialogue.

Young EDEN: This is way better than black and white!

Young EDNA: The Heckler Brothers Pictures were always the most spectacular, Eden. Look at those costumes! I had forgotten how snazzy they were.

Young EDEN: And Esmé looks even more beautiful in colour.

Young EDNA: Shhh Edie, here comes Spanky's big number. Go turn the set up so we can hear it better.

Lights dim on them, and the area in front of the screen brightens as Ronnie raises the panel in front of the SR bridge. It reveals a large face of young Spanky Bishop as The Wacky Bellhop, filling the frame. He is in the movie being watched by young Edna and young Eden. Spanky's mouth is manipulated from behind the screen by the SM. Spanky sings:

Crazydoll

Gather round now one and all
Come and meet my Crazydoll
She's a dame who's earned her fame
And my heart's back in the game
Come on kids and say her name
Come and meet my Crazydoll

Crazydoll!
She's a wacky lady
Crazydoll!
Oh yessirree
Crazydoll!
Crazy 'bout ya baby
Can't you say you're crazy for me

The music continues with a brief dance orchestration as young Eden stands up and moves directly in front of Spanky.

Young EDEN: Hey Mum, look at me! I'm a movie star too, and I'm in colour!

Young EDNA: Oh Edie!

During the following, Ronnie sings live as young Eden with the pre-recorded Spanky.

Here I am on bended knee
With the word matrimony
Please say yes that you'll be mine
Hubby's year-round Valentine
Crazy him loves crazy she
Crazydoll please marry me.

Crazydoll!
You're my little Venus
Crazydoll!
My Juliette
Crazydoll!
Nothin' comes between us
Can't you see how crazy I get?

Crazydoll!
Be my little missus
Crazydoll!
Lemme see you smile
Crazydoll!
Come and get my kisses
Crazydoll!
Oh Crazydoll!
My Crazydoll!
Take a crazy walk with me down the aisle.

Young Eden collapses into Edna's arms. They are both laughing.

Young EDNA: Oh Eden, that was wonderful! You're a regular Spanky Bishop you are!

Young EDEN: I'd rather be Esmé Massengill.

Young EDNA: Oh Edie, such a kidder. My little movie star!

Young EDEN: And you're my crazydoll Mum. Forever.

SR lights fade. Ronnie lowers the panel. CS lights restore. SR chair and marionettes are struck by the SM.

EDNA: And that's why you named her Crazydoll.

EDEN: Yeah. I remember.

EDNA: Of course you do, Edie. Your father didn't see the sense in buying that colour TV, but I held my ground. I said, "Stanley Rural, it's my family allowance, I'll spend it as I see fit!"

EDEN: Well, he never saw much sense in anything we liked.

EDNA: Edie, that's not true.

EDEN: Fine, I'm sorry I brought it up. I should know better than to criticize him in front of you.

EDNA: Oh, you're just mad at him. Just because he didn't throw his arms around you and say, "Oh, you're a homo! Isn't that just tickety-boo! Let's go have a smoke on the porch!"

EDEN: I didn't expect that. I knew he would have a hard time with it.

EDNA: Then why did you tell him, Edie? To hurt him?

EDEN: No. Maybe. I don't know.

EDNA: Well it's hard to mend a fence when you're sitting on it, Mister Man. And besides, your father isn't angry.

EDEN: Wasn't.

EDNA: What?

EDEN: Wasn't angry, not isn't.

EDNA: Don't start with me Eden.

EDEN: Mum...

EDNA: Fine. Enough. We'll have it your way. It wasn't anger. It was disappointment, that he'd have no one to pass the farm on to.

EDEN: He never even asked me if I wanted it!

EDNA: Well of course not, Edie. What would you, one of you people, want with a farm?

EDEN: There are plenty of gay farmers.

Edna pauses, shocked, then bursts into laughter.

EDNA: Oh Lord love a duck! You're pulling my leg now. Oh you! And I almost fell for it. Gay farmers!

EDEN: And ranchers.

EDNA: Eden!

EDEN: I've been to gay rodeos. Yee haw! Ride 'em cowboy!

EDNA: Now that's enough of your smart mouth! Eden, it's not nice to tease your old mum like this. Not now, what with Dolly's passing and Jesus Christ appearing in my quilt square.

EDEN: Hey Mum, did you ever think that maybe Jesus was gay?

EDNA: Now that's just talk for talk's sake Eden.

EDEN: Well, you never know. His last dinner party was men only.

EDNA: Lots of men get together for a meal. Look at the Kinsmen! Doesn't mean they're a bunch of poofs. Mind you, I've always had my suspicions about the Shriners. Something not quite right about grown men in harem pants.

Edna stands.

Now let's get Dolly buried before she starts to smell up the whole house. I'll go get my purse.

Edna exits.

EDEN: But we're just going to the backyard.

EDNA (offstage): You never know who's going to see you Eden.

EDEN: No, you never do. "Turnip Corners. Meet me there. I'm waiting. Your real Mother."

EDNA (offstage): Eden, are you coming?

EDEN: I'm already here, mother. I'm here, Esmé.

All light CS fades as Esmé music/sound theme in. Eden and the box are removed, and the drawbridge panel raised up. Crossfade into a single light on SL. It's the effect of a work lamp on a rehearsal stage, which the SM has placed a prop version of L of the SL panel. Esmé #3 walks slowly into the light. Music out.

ESMÉ: I'd forgotten how quiet you were, old friend. Not like a soundstage at all. No. That's chaos, that's dazzle, all brighter than life. Not like you, the theatre. Dark. Quiet. Secret.

She looks around her.

I grew up on you. Places like you. Long before I made my choice. Long before my life became an eternity of dark and quiet and secrets. A little girl. Just a normal little girl. A little girl who found such a dark world. "Baby Esmé—Songs and Dances From the Bible".

Esmé is hung in place in her spot. We hear music, vaguely Arabian, somewhat striptease, like the accompaniment to a silent film. Baby Esmé appears from the CSR alley entrance. She is a beautiful child, maybe five years old, dressed in a "harem" type costume. The overall image is unsettling. She dances on, gyrating seductively. Adult Esmé talks while the child version of her dances.

I played a lot of halls like this. And churches. Mother was very clever that way. They particularly liked my Salome. Dancing for the head of John the Baptist. A little girl, practically naked, dancing like a whore. Oh, they paid to watch and they loved me. The ministers' wives would cuddle me afterward and call me their living doll. Their husbands would cuddle me later, when no one else was around. Presbyterians were the worst. They always smelled damp.

Baby Esmé. Songs and Dances From the Bible.

The child dances off. Music ends.

I was pushed into the dark. Forced, by a woman who had stopped breathing in the very act of my conception. A woman who drew life from me. From what she lived through me. Yes, I wanted you, old friend. I wanted to be on the stage. And lucky for me, because I would have been pushed out here anyway.

After awhile, it was the only safe place. I knew what was lurking in the wings. In the alley. In the pulpit! And until I could figure out how to suck the life out of those who had pushed and prodded and fingered me, I stayed here. In your false, warm, protective light. My oldest friend. My saviour.

Slow musical sting of Esmé's eerie theme as the work light fades out, then a wild blast of Techno-Jesus sound and light show erupts. During this Ronnie clears Esmé and hangs her behind the SL bridge tower, the SM strikes the work light and lowers the CS drawbridge and Ronnie seats Eden in Edna's chair. There is a blast of smoke from under the CS catwalk. Light up CS and on Ronnie/Jesus above at end of transition.

JESUS: Eden.

Eden jumps up from the chair and sees him.

EDEN: Holy shit!

JESUS: Eden, we need to talk.

EDEN: This isn't real. This is not real.

JESUS: I am very real Eden.

EDEN: You don't scare me.

JESUS: Good. I'd like to see you without your fear.

EDEN: You're wasting your time. Go away.

JESUS: I can't. Your pain is what brought me here.

EDEN: Oh fuck off. If you throw that Leviticus shit in my face, I'll...

JESUS: You'll what?

EDEN: I'll come right up there and nail you, man, I swear.

JESUS: Come on, Eden!

Ronnie strikes a sudden and harsh crucifixion pose with his free hand. He catches himself and softens.

Sorry. Sorry.

EDEN: I know why you're here man, and believe me, those bombs did more good than harm.

JESUS: Eden, you're hurting people.

EDEN: I just woke them up. No one got hurt.

JESUS: Everyone got hurt.

EDEN: Oh right. We're all supposed to play by your rules.

JESUS: My rules? No one lives by my rules.

EDEN: Yeah, well, they don't work for me.

JESUS: You never even tried them.

EDEN: I did so!

JESUS: You did not!

EDEN: Did!

JESUS: Didn't!

EDEN: Yes I did!

JESUS: When?

EDEN: I went to Sunday School!

Ronnie laughs. The mood lightens somewhat.

What's so fucking funny?

JESUS: You are. You need to lighten up Eden.

EDEN: So you came here to laugh at me? Some saviour. Man, you don't even look like you. I thought you'd look, you know...

JESUS: Like a picture in Sunday School?

EDEN: Fuck off. I'm just used to the beard and long hair, okay? That looked good. Real good. I used to have such a crush on you. You were so hot. Well, him. That Sunday School Jesus. But this aging club boy thing doesn't really work on someone your age.

JESUS: I forgive you for that Eden. I thought I'd try a new image.

EDEN: Keep working on it, honey.

JESUS: Maybe you could help me.

EDEN: Let's not pretend we're pals. We have nothing in common. You're the Son of Man, I'm...I'm the son of Stan.

JESUS: So we have a lot in common. Silent fathers and saintly mothers.

EDEN: Oh please! Leave them out of it. My rage is enormous. Too big to pin on my parents. They're simple people. My rage is very complicated. And it's all mine.

JESUS: Rage is not self-contained.

EDEN: You fucking hypocrite. You peddled fear and rage yourself, didn't you? But oh, I forgot, you smoke-screened it all with magic and hocus pocus.

JESUS: Okay, yes, I thought that if people were impressed with the spectacle, maybe they'd listen. But that obviously hasn't worked out like I had hoped, so I think I need a more personal approach.

EDEN: So what are you gonna do man? Talk to people one at a time?

JESUS: Yes.

EDEN: Fuck off.

JESUS: It's true.

EDEN: Yeah right. You're gonna talk to everyone on earth, one at a time.

JESUS: I'm talking to you, aren't I?

EDEN: Well I'm not listening.

JESUS: Well I am.

EDEN: I've got nothing to say to you.

JESUS: But there's something you need to hear.

EDEN: What?

JESUS: You tell me.

EDEN: What?

JESUS: The truth.

EDEN: Man, you're a pain in the ass.

JESUS: Sorry. It's my job. Eden?

EDEN: What?

JESUS: Remember.

EDEN: What?

JESUS: When you weren't afraid.

There is a pause.

EDEN: We were playing.

JESUS: Who?

EDEN: Me and Ogden. Ogden Ramsay, the only kid in school who ever bothered with me. Well, the only boy, anyway. But that was okay. He was the only boy I noticed. He was thin and quiet and...beautiful. Not like me at all. Yet, here he was, in my house playing with me.

JESUS: Did you love him?

Eden moves to one side of the area, as if watching.

EDEN: What? No. I don't know. I was just a little kid. What did I know about love, except for what I saw in movies? We were just playing. To me, he was...someone else. It was pretend. It was all just pretend...

Special on Ronnie out. Short musical sting/memory transition. We stay in the same area, but it is now another time, years earlier. There is a subtle yet distinct lighting change to enhance this memory. A marionette of young Eden #2 runs in. He is wearing an exact replica of Edna's wedding dress. It is too big on him, and there is no veil. It is crucial that during this scene the character does not show his back to the audience. He has a purse over one arm.

Young EDEN: Okay Ogden, I'm ready. Are you ready?

OGDEN (offstage): Yeah. I guess.

Young EDEN: Well are you ready or not?

OGDEN (offstage): I'm ready. I just feel stupid Eden. What if your Mum walks in?

Young EDEN: I already told you, she's at a church meeting in town.

Ogden enters. He is, as described, a beautiful boy. He is dressed in his underclothes.

OGDEN: I guess this is what a dad would wear. It's what my Dad wears to bed.

Young EDEN: In the movies they wear silk pajamas!

OGDEN: Huh. I don't got those.

Young EDEN: It's okay. You look nice Ogden.

OGDEN: Thanks. What's that you're wearing?

Young EDEN: It's my Mum's wedding dress.

OGDEN: Do you want to be a girl?

Young EDEN: No.

OGDEN: Then why are you dressed like one?

Young EDEN: I'm not dressed like a girl. I'm dressed like a star!

OGDEN: You want to be a star?

Young EDEN:	Yes.
OGDEN:	But you're dressed like a girl star.
Young EDEN:	The only stars are girl stars.
OGDEN:	Then you want to be a girl.
Young EDEN:	I dunno. No.
OGDEN:	Doesn't matter. You look nice Eden. What's in the purse?
Young EDEN:	Nothing.
OGDEN:	Then why do you have it?
Young EDEN:	'Cause I like it. It goes.
OGDEN:	So, what should I call you?
Young EDEN:	I dunno. You could call me...your wife.

OGDEN: Nah, that's weird.

Young EDEN: Yeah. That's weird.

OGDEN: I know. I'll call you...purse boy!

Young EDEN: Okay.

Suddenly a strong, harsh backlight shines on Ronnie on the CS bridge. He is Stanley Rural. The light outlines his size, massive compared to the two small boys beneath.

OGDEN: It's your Dad!

STANLEY: Go home, Ogden.

OGDEN: We were just playing.

STANLEY: Put your clothes on and go home, Ogden.

OGDEN: Yes, Mr. Rural.

He starts to exit, then turns to Eden.

See ya, Eden.

STANLEY: Now!

Ogden exits.

STANLEY: What are you doing, boy?

Young EDEN: Nothing. Honest. Playing.

STANLEY: Playing? What?

Young EDEN: Nothing. Wedding.

STANLEY: Wedding?

Young EDEN: I was being...

STANLEY: Who?

Young EDEN: Mum. I was Mum, Dad.

STANLEY: Come here.

Young EDEN: Except she was like a movie star.

STANLEY: Come here.

Young EDEN: And Ogden was sort of...you Daddy.

STANLEY: Take that dress off and come here. Now!

Young EDEN: No, we were just playing.

STANLEY: How dare you touch that dress, you little bastard.

Young EDEN: I'll put it away Daddy. Just like I found it.

STANLEY: Come here.

Young EDEN: No...

He starts to move.

STANLEY: I said come here!

Ronnie grabs the strings of the marionette and violently pulls the puppet of young Eden up to his level.

Look at you. Look at...this. Eden, the spoiled fruit!

Young EDEN: Daddy, no! Please Daddy!

Music sting. Short, brutal, loud. Young Eden is "thrown" down to the stage level, bent over the chair and facing upstage, revealing the bloodstained back of the wedding dress.

EDEN: My mother's wedding dress was covered in blood. And I had lost the only man I ever loved. I hated him for that.

Young Eden exits slowly.

And that's when I learned the power of rage.

Eden sits in the chair.

JESUS: Eden...

EDEN: Leave me alone. I have nothing to say to you.

Ronnie sits on the CS catwalk, feet dangling into Eden's playing area. Crossfade from top light to catwalk light. He sings:

JESUS: **Midnight in Monte Carlo**

All I remember
Is midnight and moonlight
You're but a ghost in the mist
All I remember is
Midnight and moonlight
Starlight and candles
Champagne and whispers
And then

Am I right?
I'm kissed at midnight
With the heavens aglow
I was kissed at midnight in Monte Carlo

EDEN: You know that?

JESUS: "Midnight in Monte Carlo". Gloria Cartier was one of Esmé's best performances.

EDEN: Fuck off, you know Esmé?

JESUS: I've been watching her for years. Just like you.

EDEN: That's so wild.

JESUS: Not really. See Eden, we aren't that different.

EDEN: She's my blood.

JESUS: I am your blood.

EDEN: No man, she's my mother.

JESUS: What?

EDEN: That's why she's here. I got a note. She wants to meet me.

JESUS: Oh Eden, no.

EDEN: I'm finally going to meet my birth mother and she's Esmé Massengill!

JESUS: Eden, I wouldn't do that if I were you.

EDEN: Well, you're not me, are you? See, we don't have a bloody thing in common.

Techno-Jesus music transition begins. Light out CS. Ronnie hangs Eden backstage and the SM raises the CS drawbridge panel. SL acting area light comes up. The panel stays down, and there are no furniture props. Ronnie walks Fluffer onstage. Music ends.

FLUFFER: Okay everyone, places please for rehearsal. We'll start at the top of Act Two. I need Mr. Bishop onstage in costume as Joseph. Places please.

Spanky enters. He is dressed as Joseph, with long robes and sandals. He's running lines.

SPANKY: Okay Mary, lemme get this straight. When we got

married, you were a virgin. Right? Now all of a sudden you tell me you're with child. *Bist meshugeh* (are you crazy)? I haven't even touched you! Believe me, a man remembers details like that.

FLUFFER: Bravo Mr. Bishop! I think you finally have that speech nailed.

SPANKY: Thank you, Fluffer. And where is my delightful co-star?

FLUFFER: Oh, Miss Massengill is just getting into her Virgin Mary costume.

Esmé #4 enters from SL wearing her Mary costume. This looks nothing at all like the Virgin Mary, but instead is a scanty Ziegfeld-like concoction of beads and feathers. With fishnets.

ESMÉ: Sorry to keep you waiting darlings, but the duct tape on my ass keeps slipping. Fluffer, make a note to bone my *derrière* after rehearsal.

FLUFFER: Um, sure thing Miss M.

ESMÉ: Is something wrong Fluffer? What are you staring at?

FLUFFER: That certainly is a lot of cleavage for the Virgin Mary, Miss Massengill.

ESMÉ: She was pregnant darling. Her tits would have been enormous.

FLUFFER: Oh. Do you need a pillow for pregnancy padding?

ESMÉ: Padding? When will you learn Fluffer? I'm not an actress, I'm a star!

FLUFFER: But you just said she was pregnant.

ESMÉ: Well it's not a literal interpretation. Allow me some license. Christ, it's a musical!

FLUFFER: Sorry, Miss Massengill, I just thought that...

ESMÉ: No one cares what you think, you stupid dyke.

FLUFFER: I am not a dyke. I am a professional stage manager from Toronto.

ESMÉ: Oh excuse me. I wasn't aware that there was a difference! Now please, let's get on with it.

FLUFFER: Okay, let's take it from the top of the flight scene.

Places please.

Fluffer moves aside to SL and Esmé and Spanky take CS.

When you're ready Mr. Bishop.

SPANKY/Joseph: *Oy* Mary, it's true I tell you. What, I should lie to you about such a thing? May God strike me dead I should lie to my wife. I should *plotz* right before you, a lie crosses my lips. There was this angel. Gorgeous! A blonde *shikse* angel. She comes to me, a vision I tell you, and she says, "Joseph, get your wife and your ass outta town. Herod, that *schmuk*, he's killing all the babies." *Oy vey Is mier!* Just when you get yourself *shtupped* by the big guy, such a decree!

ESMÉ/Mary: But Joe, my crazy madcap Joe, where oh where will we go?

SPANKY/Joseph: To Egypt my darling! We'll leave this *farkuckt* place and find peace. Mind you, given your condition Mary, it appears you already found a piece!

ESMÉ: Spanky! That's not in the script!

SPANKY: I know, but it gets a laugh.

ESMÉ: Fine. Whatever. Enough! Let's just skip to the duet.

FLUFFER: Oh no oh no oh no, we can't!

ESMÉ: No? Why not, Fluffer?

FLUFFER: Because three of the band members are missing.

ESMÉ: Three? Spanky!

SPANKY: Don't look at me.

ESMÉ: Spanky...

SPANKY: Honest. Here, check my breath.

He breathes, wheezing, onto her.

ESMÉ: Fine. Where's Uta?

SPANKY: I thought she was with you.

ESMÉ: No. Well don't just stand there, go find her! And get her into costume. We have to rework the angel sequence without the German Tourette's Syndrome.

SPANKY: I warned you about taking her on the road.

ESMÉ: What was I to do? Lock her in her casket? I owe her everything!

SPANKY: *Oy*, for such a life we're thankful?

He exits.

ESMÉ: Let's get on with it Fluffer. We'll rehearse my solo. The show-stopping road to Bethlehem number, "My Ass is Killing Me". Where's the donkey?

The SM places a chair onstage which has a prop donkey head made from a sock attached to it.

Fluffer, what's that?

FLUFFER: Your ass. I made it myself!

ESMÉ: Obviously. I thought I was getting real livestock!

FLUFFER: Oh no oh no oh no! People are very protective of their animals ever since fourteen cows were found mutilated and drained of all their blood!

ESMÉ: Damn that Uta! I need a drink!

Esmé exits R.

FLUFFER: But Miss Massengill, it's not time for an Equity break yet. Oh no. Well, the show must go on.

Fluffer looks around, strokes the prop donkey head, and begins "acting".

Oh Joe, oh Joe, my crazy madcap Joe! Looking for a room to let, but everyone says oh no, oh no, oh no!

ESMÉ
(offstage): Fluffer!

FLUFFER: Coming!

Fluffer runs off. Lights out SL. During the following voice-over, Ronnie hangs Esmé and Fluffer backstage while the SM strikes the donkey chair prop and lowers the CS drawbridge panel. Ronnie places Eden #1 in Edna's chair, and Edna #1 standing SL of him.

ANNOUNCER/
Male Voice
(recorded): In other news, city police report that there are no new developments in the Purse Boy Bombings. While many community leaders are pointing fingers at the Prairie Revival Party for the rash of bombings targeted at gay and lesbian businesses, an unconfirmed source hints that this may be the work of a homosexual person. This comment has inflamed gay rights activists who denounce it as continued fear-mongering from the Prairie Revival Party.

Light up on CS.

EDNA: Lord love a duck, who would do such a thing?

EDEN: Me.

EDNA: Oh Edie!

EDEN: It's true. I did it.

EDNA: There you go again with your teasing, Mister Man.

EDEN: Don't you remember Mum? What kids used to yell at me. What they called me?

There is a pause as Edna remembers. She speaks softly:

EDNA: Purse Boy.

EDEN: Yeah, Purse Boy. See, it's me. I did it, Mum.

EDNA: Lord love a duck. What would your father say about this?

EDEN: Why don't you ask him Mum?

EDNA: Don't be cheeky.

EDEN: I'm not. You talk to him every day, don't you?

EDNA: He's my husband.

EDEN: Was.

EDNA: Is.

EDEN: Mum...

EDNA: Eden, don't start! Not this. Not now.

EDEN: Mum, please.

EDNA: What do you want from me Eden? Why have you come home? To upset me? To make fun of me?

EDEN: No. I came to find myself.

EDNA: You think too much. Find yourself. Lord love a duck! You know who you are.

EDEN: No, I don't.

EDNA: Well I know who you are Edie. You're my son.

EDEN: No I'm not.

EDNA: What?

EDEN: I'm someone else's son.

EDNA: No! You're my son. I may not have given you life, but I gave you my life. And I've nothing left to give Eden.

EDEN: How about the truth? Come on Mum, say it. Please. Please Mum. Damn you, say it!

Silence. Edna turns away. She sits.

Yeah, well. I guess that says it all.

Eden leaves, walking to the SR area where he is hung from the gallows. He is in dim light during Edna's following monologue. Her light CS has become that of an inner dialogue/dream-state. Not dim, just not "real".

EDNA: We sold the farm in 1988. Not because Eden didn't want it. Four years before, my Stanley took ill. A heart attack. It seems that all those years of my sensible prairie cooking had not sustained my man as intended, but instead, clogged his arteries to the point where his well-hidden heart simply could not get the blood it needed.

There were four or five important moments in our married life. Our wedding day. The time we were told I could not have children. The occasion of Eden coming into our home and our lives. And this. They weren't all happy, they were just important. And Stanley's illness was very important.

The "Jesus special" light comes up on Ronnie's face atop the CS bridge.

JESUS: The important moments live on because they live within love.

EDNA: Jesus, dear, I'm trying to tell a story. Now if you insist on interrupting I'll never get through it.

JESUS: Sorry, Edna. What was I thinking. Mind if I listen?

EDNA: Suit yourself.

Ronnie's special out.

Stanley needed an operation. I have never been so afraid in all my life. Stanley saw it all as just a nuisance, like a piece of machinery that was screwy but you didn't have time to fix. I made him make time. And he made me promise not to worry. Nothing to worry about, he'd say. Government health care and the Red Cross. Stanley said you couldn't be in better hands.

So, on October 13, 1984 Stanley had a triple bypass. It was risky, but the doctor tried to make me think it was all going to go just tickity-boo. What none of us expected, including the doctor, was that Stanley would have another heart attack once they had him on the table, which is exactly what happened.

There was a lot of bleeding that complicated matters. To this day I still don't understand all the fancy medical words, but what we learned later was that he had been injected with a clotting agent made from blood the morning after surgery to stop the bleeding. And as bad as it had all been, within a week Stanley seemed to be on the road to recovery. And courtesy of medical science, government health care and the Red Cross, I brought my man home.

But Stanley never had the new lease on life you hear others talk about. There was no new awakening of his spirit, no realisation of the good fortune of having a second chance. I think he realised that while his life wasn't over, the life he had always known had changed. And my Stanley did not like change. He's an Albertan. Change disappointed him.

But that man is the other half of my velcro. And whether he admitted it or not, he needed me. And I finally realised how much I needed him.

Light crossfades from CS to SR.

EDEN: July 1986, my father was back in the hospital. His heart was fine. It was pneumonia. Pneumonia in July. PCP. It was a symptom I had heard of many times.

My father had not spoken to me much since the infamous Thanksgiving jellied salad coming out party. Not that he had spoken to me much before that. I grew up in a household where silence really was golden. No one spoke. Ever, except to say "Pass the potatoes". I guess that's why the movies became so important to me. Up there, on the screen, was a world of people doing the strangest thing. They were talking. To one another. And sometimes, it felt like they were talking to me.

A pool of light comes up on the SR catwalk. Young Esmé #4 enters, dressed in another dazzling gown. She "acts" alone, playing the scene with an unseen man. Eden remains facing front. He doesn't need to watch it, it's in his head.

ESMÉ/Amanda: Rex, before I leave you—and I am leaving you, Rex—there's something you must know.

REX/Male Voice: You can't leave me Amanda. I love you, woman!

ESMÉ/Amanda: But I don't love you. I've never loved you, Rex!

REX/Male Voice: Amanda!

ESMÉ/Amanda: No, Rex, don't! Our liaison was madness, beating like a heart, but without blood. Passionless. Let me go, Rex, let me go!

REX/Male Voice: Then go. Go to him! That's it, isn't it? There's someone else, isn't there, Amanda? Who is he? I'll kill the varmint!

ESMÉ/Amanda: No! For without him I will die!

REX/Male Voice: Who is he, Amanda? Answer me!

ESMÉ/Amanda: He's my one true love! My Eden!

She turns to Eden and beckons to him.

Eden, come to me. I have so much to tell you.

EDEN: I went to see my father in the hospital. I got as far as the doorway to his ward. He saw me standing there. And turned his head and looked out the window. I left, without saying a word.

ESMÉ: Eden, come home.

Young Esmé exits and is hung up. Lights down on Eden, and crossfade up again on Edna as Ronnie crosses to the CS bridge.

EDNA: I thought it was awfully queer, a man like Stanley getting pneumonia in the summer. But the doctor said he was just run down. And sure enough, in three weeks my man was home again. I don't think Eden even considered coming home, but he phoned. He phoned almost every day. He phoned every day and kept pestering me to get some blood tests done on his father. He wouldn't let up on that, day after day. I finally just had to tell him, Lord love a duck Edie, we've got a medical doctor, government health care

and the blessed Red Cross on our side. I think if we needed a bunch of fancy tests they would have let us know by now.

It was the one time he hung up on me.

But Christmas of that year, our family was together again. I worked like a madwoman! I loved Christmas. And Eden gave me the most wonderful present. A puppy! Called her Crazydoll, after one of those old Esmé Massengill movies. Can you imagine that? A dog named after a movie! I called her Dolly. She was a frisky bundle that Christmas day, but she brought some life back into this house.

And that night, Stanley even started feeling a little perky. You know, down there. Whispered to me in bed, "Edna, I got another present for you". I said to him, Lord love a duck Mr. Stanley Rural, what in Sam Hill are you thinking? I've got turkey gas something terrible! But he was gentle. I don't remember him ever being so gentle on top of me. Maybe it was his condition. Maybe it was out of respect for my gas. Whatever it was, I felt like his wife again. No. I felt like his partner. We'd get through this.

Christmas 1986. I thought I was so happy.

Light up again on Eden SR and down CS.

EDEN: Boxing Day my father got sick. We already knew the symptoms, so it was just a matter of getting him to the hospital so they could tell us it was the pneumonia again. It was the one and only time in my life I saw my mother angry. I walked into the kitchen late that night, and in the dark, with only the opened refrigerator for light, I saw her standing at the table with a knife in her hand. She was stabbing the left-over turkey carcass, over and over. Not crying, not screaming, just stabbing. And with each plunge of the knife she whispered, "Happy birthday, happy birthday, happy birthday". At some point I must have moved or she realised I was there, watching. Without turning, without stopping her stabbing, she just said

CS light up.

EDNA: Go to bed Edie. This is between me and him.

EDEN: I went to the hospital the following day. To forgive my father. To ask him to forgive me. But in true Rural fashion, not a word was spoken. I didn't make it on time.

EDNA: I've never said good-bye to my Stanley. I couldn't bear to live in this house alone.

EDEN: We greeted 1987 with a funeral. And the results of an autopsy, which I had insisted on. It was exactly what I had known all along. I guess the only saving grace was that Mum and Dad were so old that, well, you know, at least she wasn't at risk.

EDNA: After all those years of married life, I can't let him go. He's inside of me. He is my blood.

EDEN: But we don't talk about it. It's not the kind of thing anyone would believe anyway. Not in Turnip Corners. Fuck this town. Fuck this family. I'm going to meet Esmé. I am her blood.

Eden exits. His light goes out. Edna is very still.

EDNA: Alright. If it's so important, I'll say it for you Eden. Your father... My husband, Stanley Rural, is dead. He died of complications brought about by AIDS.

Pause.

I said it out loud. I said it out loud, Eden.

She stands.

Eden?

Light slowly fades on Edna CS. She is hung backstage. Music transition. Ronnie makes his way to SL bridge. He slowly raises the SL panel, revealing Eden #3, nude and hung on a cross à la the crucifixion. This is a special figure, fastened to the cross and with a modified control for moving only Eden's head, which is operated from behind by the SM. Smoke and light inside the bridge tower. Esmé #5 enters from the SR side of the SL area and stands before him.

EDEN: Why are you doing this to me?

ESMÉ: I could have impaled you on a stake like my predecessor, Vlad, but we vampires have such an aversion to stakes.

She laughs.

EDEN: But this. The cross. You can't look at it, not if you're a vampire.

ESMÉ: Dear boy, you are so damaged by Hollywood. Once, yes, the sign of the cross was repellent to us. Back when people believed in him. Believed in the possibility of his redemption. But no one really believes in him anymore, so the imagery is benign.

EDEN: But he's here.

ESMÉ: Of course. And you've seen him. But do you believe in him, even now?

Eden is silent.

Precisely. Oh, he and I have so much in common.

EDEN: What? You're a monster and he's...

ESMÉ: Yes?

EDEN: He's him.

ESMÉ: And we're both cursed by a public far more interested in the myth of us, rather than the reality. You know, seeing you on the cross, like he was so long ago, makes me think I should put the crucifixion scene back in the show. Poor Mary, sobbing her ass off at the base of the cross.

EDEN: Please. Don't do this. Not to me. I've loved you my whole life.

ESMÉ: Well your whole life has been shit! You don't have a life. What, you think you're special? A lonely little faggot who lived his life through movies? Darling, that's neither a life nor special. That's common. That's boring. That's general fucking public. You could have done something. Been somebody. But no, you let me do all the work while you watched. Well sweetie, now I'm watching you. Die.

EDEN: But you're my...

ESMÉ: What? Your mother?

EDEN: You said so.

ESMÉ: No, you believed so. I just didn't deny it.

EDEN: Why not?

ESMÉ: Because I'm hungry! I'm always hungry. And there's always one of you around. So willing to please me. To feed me.

EDEN: I wanted you to be my mother.

ESMÉ: Well I'm not, so get over it. You already have a perfectly good mother. A woman so good not even I would fuck with her. But that didn't stop you, did it darling?

EDEN: No. She is perfectly good, isn't she?

ESME: How lovely. You've had your redeeming moment of insight before dying.

EDEN: No. Please, I want to live!

ESMÉ: You are so dreary. I said that line first! When I played Sissy Mink, an innocent society dame framed for murder in "Cell-Block Celebrity". Listen to you. You're pathetic. You even steal from me when you're begging for your life. There's nothing original about you.

Spanky #1 enters.

SPANKY: Esmé, we got trouble.

He sees Eden on the cross.

What's this? I thought we cut the crucifixion scene.

ESMÉ: Spanky darling, join me for a drink?

SPANKY: Who is this?

ESMÉ: A fan. He was dying to meet me.

SPANKY: Why this, Esmé? Why now? We got Jesus Christ in town, he's watching us, and you do this? You think this is funny? You push too far, Esmé. We already got enough trouble on our hands.

ESMÉ: A few dead cattle. Relax Spanky. They'll just blame it on aliens, like always.

SPANKY: Uta's running all over town feeding on the locals!

ESMÉ: What? Well did you catch her?

SPANKY: I'm an old man, I haven't fed in days. Now you want I should run a marathon after a crazy blood-drunk Hun?

ESMÉ: Fine! I'll go.

She starts to exit, then turns back. She looks first at Eden, then to Spanky.

Oh, and Spanky, if this one dies while I'm out, don't worry. The little faggot was empty to begin with.

She exits.

EDEN: Please...

SPANKY: Shhh, don't talk. It's easier that way.

EDEN: Please...

SPANKY: Kid, don't get me involved. Please.

Eden is faint and delirious. He starts to sing, softly.

EDEN: "Gather round now one and all..."

SPANKY: What did you say?

EDEN: "Come and meet my Crazydoll..."

SPANKY: Well I'll be.

EDEN: "She's a dame who's earned her fame..."

SPANKY: "And my heart's back in the game
Come on kids and say her name
Come and meet my crazy Crazydoll"

EDEN: Hi, Mr. Bishop.

SPANKY: Who are you, kid?

EDEN: I'm Eden. Eden...Rural.

SPANKY: Rural? Say, this Edna Rural, the one with the Shroud protecting her...you related?

EDEN: Yes. She's my...Crazydoll.

SPANKY: Oy. This is some situation you got yourself into my friend. It may be too late, but come on, let's get you home.

He moves toward the cross, close to Eden.

EDEN: Are you going to feed on me too?

SPANKY: Nah, you're a good kid, I can tell.

EDEN: How?

SPANKY: Trust me, I got a nose for these things.

Lights dim as Spanky's hands reach up to Eden. Music transition in. Ronnie lowers the SL panel and crosses to CS bridge. CS drawbridge down. Light slowly comes up on Edna. She is in her nightie and robe. Spanky stands SL of her.

EDNA: Mr. Bishop, there's a lot I don't understand in this world, and I don't understand any of this. But I thank you. Because I know, somehow, you didn't have to bring my boy home to me.

SPANKY: I heard you were a good woman, Edna Rural. Terrible things happen in the world, I know. But family, that's important. And I thought maybe this terrible thing shouldn't happen to yours, Edna Rural.

EDNA: It's too late for that I'm afraid.

SPANKY: I'm sorry.

EDNA: Don't be. Everything happens for a reason, I'm sure. And if there's one thing I am, Mr. Bishop, it's positive.

SPANKY: I could tell.

EDNA: Oh? How?

SPANKY: I got a nose for these things. Edna Rural, I'm a vampire!

EDNA: Oh yeah, eh?

SPANKY: You're not afraid?

EDNA: Children fear creatures of the night, Mr. Bishop. When you're an adult, you learn to fear the monsters that live in daylight.

SPANKY: I've seen these monsters.

EDNA: Why would you give up Hollywood stardom for such a life, Mr. Bishop?

SPANKY: Please, it's Spanky.

EDNA: Spanky.

SPANKY: Because I had a rage, Edna Rural, not unlike your Eden. And when Uta and Esmé offered me this life, I embraced it as my passport to vengeance.

EDNA: But you were Spanky Bishop! Everyone loved you.

SPANKY: My dear lady, even when I was larger than life on the screen, there were many people who hated me. Who hated what I was.

EDNA: Who could hate The Wacky Bellhop?

Spanky sits in Edna's chair as SM climbs onto the SL bridge.

SPANKY: We started hearing rumours around the lot. At first, vague threads, nothing concrete. Jews were being shipped away overseas. We were used to being hated, nothing news in that. A writer on contract with the studio, his family still in Europe, he cracks one day in his bungalow. Shoots himself in the head. Of course the studio covered it up. Said he was a drunk. Edna Rural, I'm telling you, I barely knew the man, but he was no drunk. He had sent someone money to get his wife and kids out, but they're not there. The apartment is in shambles. Gone. Shipped, like cattle. I ask you Edna Rural, what person wouldn't go crazy with such news?

EDNA: Lord love a duck.

Ronnie hangs Spanky and Edna onstage and crosses to the SL tower. The SM hands him a pair of sunglasses, which he puts on, and the marionette of Young Spanky dressed as The Wacky Bellhop. Lights crossfade, down on CS and up SL on Young Spanky. Front light on Ronnie in sunglasses above. During the following speech, he is the studio boss.

SPANKY: So I go to the studio bosses, straight from the set. I say we gotta do something. All of a sudden, the door closes, things get serious. They say to me, "Spanky", they say, "it's true. They're killing all the Jews." So I say we gotta tell someone. And they say to me me, "Tell who, Spanky?" The government, our government! "Spanky," they tell me, "the government knows. They don't care." Then the people. We gotta tell the people! "How would we do that Spanky? How would we convince people of such fantastic horror?" You're in the movie business, I scream. You sell horror and fantasy and craziness to people everyday. Make a newsreel. Tell the people!

Ronnie flips sunglasses up as he speaks for Edna and (old) Spanky.

EDNA: Good for you, Spanky, good for you!

SPANKY: Good for me? Who was I? I was nobody.

EDNA: You were Spanky Bishop.

Sunglasses down again.

SPANKY: No. I was Schmool Bischovsky, the low serf of low slapschtick from the lower East side. Hollywood made me Spanky Bishop, to the world. But to them, I was still just Schmool Bischovsky. And they said to me, "Spanky, don't make trouble. Don't make waves. People don't want to hear about this. And they don't want to hear bad news from a goofy looking Jew like you. Be funny, Spanky. The world loves you when you're funny. We love you...when you're funny". And with that, the meeting was over.

Light on Ronnie out as he hands sunglasses to the SM.

EDNA: That's terrible.

SPANKY: What's terrible, Edna Rural, is that these were Jews saying this to me. The Heckler Brothers themselves, telling me to keep my mouth shut. I just couldn't be funny anymore. It was over for me.

SL light out. Ronnie hands Young Spanky to SM and crosses back to centre bridge as light CS restores.

EDNA: I'm confused.

SPANKY: Don't worry, it's part of your charm.

EDNA: No, I mean why did you become a vampire?

SPANKY: To kill the monsters of daylight. To kill Nazis. But there were too many, even for a thirst like mine. Eight million members of the Nazi party. Eight million guilty Germans with blood on their hands.

EDNA: But isn't Miss Häagen-Daz a German?

SPANKY: Uta is an actress. And once a great star. We came alive at night, drinking the applause of our audience. You get drunk on that, addicted, but it's a fix you need daily. Long before this life, I was already a vampire of sorts. Not many people understand that. But Uta did. So you see Edna Rural, to me she's family.

EDNA: It's too bad you didn't know that earlier, Spanky.

SPANKY: What?

EDNA: That family isn't always about blood.

SPANKY: Edna Rural, do an old man a favour. End it. Drive a stake through my heart!

EDNA: Oh Spanky, not in the living room!

SPANKY: Please Edna Rural. I can't go on. I'm finished!

EDNA: Listen to you. Finished! Shame on you Spanky, shame on you. Why, there are lots of monsters still walking free. Getting away with murder in broad daylight, with blood on their hands. And too much unfinished business that no government commission or inquiry will ever set it right. Lord love a duck, we need solutions with some teeth in them. So you get up, Spanky. Get up and go on. Go on for my Eden. Go on for me.

SPANKY: You're one hell of a woman, Edna Rural. I'd kiss you, but I got my teeth in.

EDNA: Just tell me one last thing, Spanky.

SPANKY: Anything for you, Edna Rural.

EDNA: What does "*oy*" mean?

SPANKY: *Oy*. Well, it's like what you say, Edna Rural. "Lord love a duck".

EDNA: Well lord love a duck! Good luck, Spanky Bishop.

SPANKY: Good luck, Edna Rural.

They embrace. Spanky exits left and is hung up backstage.

EDNA: Happy hunting! And Spanky...go east.

Eden #4 enters R, dressed in pajamas and a robe. His neck is bandaged.

EDEN: Mum?

EDNA: Eden, *oy!* What are you doing up? Go back to bed!

EDEN: I need to tell you something.

EDNA: Later, you're too weak.

EDEN: No, now.

EDNA: Alright then, but you come sit down.

He sits in the chair.

EDEN: I thought Esmé Massengill was my mother. You know, my birth mother.

EDNA: Oh Eden. You've watched too many movies, dear.

EDEN: I should have just asked you, but you never wanted to

talk about it. You were so ashamed that I was adopted.

EDNA: Is that what you think?

EDEN: Yes.

EDNA: Oh Eden, no. No. I was always so proud of you. That you were my little boy.

EDEN: Really?

EDNA: Eden, most people who can have children are stuck with what life hands them. Your father and me got a special baby. It's like...well, you know when you go to the IGA and want to buy a roast? The butcher doesn't just hand you any old piece of meat. No, he puts them all on display and lets you choose the best one. Well, that's what your father and me did. We chose the prime cut. We chose you, Edie.

EDEN: Mum, you're so weird. I always thought you were ashamed of me because I wasn't part of you.

EDNA: You are a part of me. But Eden, it was different when I was younger. We didn't have the talk shows telling us how to think or what was right. We had something worse. Ladies' Church Groups. A bunch of mean-spirited women who said one thing to your face and another behind your back. And if you couldn't have a baby, those holier-than-thou mothers looked at you as if you were broken. They whispered things about you. They made you—they made me—feel less than a whole woman.

It's true Edie, I couldn't talk about this because I was ashamed. But not of you. Of me. I'm ashamed of broken, barren Edna.

EDEN: You're not broken. You're a beautiful woman.

EDNA: Listen to you, bending my ear like some Carlo Biscotti in a movie! No Edie, I'm just a silly old biddy in a Sears housecoat. But your mother, the woman who brought you into this world, she was beautiful.

EDEN: Mum, you don't have to do this.

EDNA: Yes, I do. I'm tired, Edie. Tired of secrets. You should know. It's true.

EDEN: What Mum?

EDNA: That your mother was the most beautiful gal in all of Turnip Corners.

EDEN: You knew her?

EDNA: She was my maid of honor.

EDEN: Miss Pickles?

EDNA: Cora Jean. As lovely as those ballerinas in a wind up jewellery case.

Light CS dims and comes up SL. Edna and Eden are hung onstage as Ronnie goes to Cora Jean at the bandstand. As he crosses, he takes a black toque from the SM. There is xylophone music during the scene, although Cora Jean does not play it herself. She leaves the instrument and steps off the bandstand as Edna continues talking.

After your father and I got married, Cora Jean took the train to Winnipeg. It was big news in Turnip Corners, one of our own going off to the city. Winnipeg and the ballet! It all seemed so exotic then. We knew she would make something of herself.

Cora Jean dances for a moment, then stops as the music becomes darker.

But the real world outside isn't as sugar coated as the ballets that lived inside her mind. But Cora Jean didn't know that. She was always off in her beautiful world. Always seeing painted scenery in front of her eyes, not reality. And so of course she didn't see him. Even when he was practically beside her, I don't think she ever knew he was there.

EDEN: Who?

EDNA: The man. Some man. Walking home from her class one night, Cora Jean was...raped.

Ronnie yanks the toque onto his head and jumps down off the bridge, standing in the alley between the SL side tower and the SL bridge. He is the man. As the music reaches its strange, violent crescendo, he grabs the puppet. There is a scream—Cora Jean's—and he covers her mouth. Saturated red light and music peak as Ronnie thrusts forward. He releases Cora, spits on her, quickly climbs back on the bridge and removes the toque.

Beaten and raped by a man she never knew, and never saw again. And I don't think she ever saw that beautiful scenery in her mind again.

Cora Jean walks slowly off in the alley between the SL side tower and bridge. Ronnie crosses to the CS bridge as light restores there.

She came home. It was kept quiet. Everyone knew, but not a word was spoken, not even in private. But when her time came, I sat with her. I owed her that. I don't know if she recognised me, but she squeezed my hand and stared at me the whole time. She was quiet so long, it's like a dream ended when that baby came out hollerin'. You woke me up from that dream Eden. I was the first person to hold you. And I named you. Eden. Because what was barren had become bountiful.

EDEN: That was you in the light.

EDNA: Poor Cora Jean. I don't even think she remembers.

EDEN: Yes, she does. She sent me a note.

EDNA: No, Eden. I sent you that note.

EDEN: You? Why?

EDNA: Because I was so lonely, with your father gone and Dolly dying. I needed you, Edie. I may not be your flesh and blood, but you're my heart and soul. I knew you wouldn't come home just to see me, but I thought you might come to her. Your mother. Your beautiful mother.

There is a moment of silence, then Eden places a hand on Edna's arm.

EDEN: You are my mother. My only mother. And I am your son. Tell anyone who thinks differently to fuck off.

EDNA: Eden!

EDEN: Mum, tell them.

EDNA: Eden, don't.

EDEN: Mum, I'm really sick. So I need you to promise me you'll tell them to fuck off. Promise?

EDNA: I promise.

EDEN: Then say it.

EDNA: Eden...

EDEN: Please Mum. Say it out loud. If you're proud, it's not a secret and they can't use it against you anymore.

Edna is silent, then slowly:

EDNA: This is my son. And I... I am not a broken woman. So fuck off, you church bitches!

EDEN: That's my girl!

EDNA: Now you do something for me.

EDEN: Anything for you, Crazydoll.

EDNA: Stop being so angry.

EDEN: I can't. I'm filled with rage.

EDNA: Eden, that's not rage. It's disappointment. The curse of the Rural men.

EDEN: Forgive me, Mum.

EDNA: It's not my forgiveness you need dear. You know what you have to do.

EDEN: Oh Mum, come on. You don't believe in that.

EDNA: Eden, he's in town. It won't hurt to ask!

Eden looks up.

EDEN: Hey. Are you up there? I'm sorry.

Light on Ronnie's face.

JESUS: I don't need your apology, Eden.

EDNA: He wants your forgiveness. Give it to him.

JESUS: He already has it, Edna. What do you expect me to do?

EDNA: What do I expect? I expect you to heal him. That's what you do, isn't it?

JESUS: Sometimes, yes.

EDNA: Yes, sometimes. When you feel like it. When you need some attention. I guess you didn't care for any publicity when Spanky's people were being herded off like cattle. A bit too messy for you, dear? Where were you during the Holocaust? Funny, I thought you were a Jew. Didn't you need attention when Cora Jean was raped? Didn't you hear her screams? Obviously you didn't need attention when my Stanley was dying. Oh no, he was... what was he to you? You and your cross. Your bloody Red Cross! What was my man then? A sacrifice? An example? I am talking to you! I've talked to you my whole life and you never answered me. Well you're in my house now mister and you will answer to me!

JESUS: I'm sorry I disappoint you, Edna.

EDNA: I am not disappointed, don't you accuse me of that! I'm angry at you. My boy is ill. And you can fix it, in the twinkling of an eye. Well then do it. Heal him. Why do you want him so soon? Why now? You took my man, you took my dog, well take me next, but not my son. I'm not like your family. Your father. I can't watch my boy suffer and die just to teach a lesson that no one will ever learn.

JESUS: Let him learn peace, Edna. With me.

EDNA: Peace? You've got some cheek waltzing into this house and using that word, mister! All the slaughtering and hatred and sacrifice made in your name. You call that peace? Once I thought all paths led to you, but I see you for what you really are. You're nothing. Nothing more than a road of sadness. Of despair. Damn you! Damn you and your street of blood!

JESUS: Stop blaming me! I'm tired of being blamed for everything. I'm not to blame. Eden started this, Edna, not me. All I can offer him is the road home.

EDNA: Well that's not good enough for me! Shame on you. I wonder what your mother would think of you now.

She turns away. Eden looks up.

EDEN: I'm sorry.

JESUS: Shut up, Eden.

Young Eden #2, wearing the wedding dress, appears in the alley between the SR and CS bridges.

Tell him.

EDEN: Who is that?

JESUS: It's Purse Boy. Washed in blood. Tell him.

EDEN: I'm sorry.

Young EDEN: I forgive you.

Young Eden exits. Intro to "Behold, The Blessed Prairie" starts as underscore.

EDEN: I forgave myself. Mum? Mum!

EDNA: Shhh, Eden, it's alright.

EDEN: Mum, where am I?

EDNA: Oh Edie. You're home.

Edna sings to him softly.

Behold, the Blessed Prairie

At dusk the dormant sky turns flame
A gentle breeze stirs wild again
And all around the eyes can see
How this our land is strong and free
Let us rejoice, with grateful voice
Behold
Behold

Eden sings the last line.

EDEN: Behold, the blessed prairie

EDNA: Sure is nice to hear you sing again, mister.

EDEN: Mum?

EDNA: Yes dear?

EDEN: I'm not afraid.

EDNA: That's good Edie, that's real good.

Eden gasps quietly, thrusting forward a bit, then slumps back into the chair. He is dead. Edna holds him close.

My little boy.

The tableau is held for a moment, then lights snap out CS and up on Ronnie's Jesus special above.

JESUS: Esmé!

Special snaps out as the "Techno Jesus" sound and light show begins again. Ronnie clears the two marionettes and strikes the gallows hanging rods as he crosses to the SR side tower. The SM places a duplicate cross DSL and hangs (a short-strung) Esmé #6 in front of the SL panel. Ronnie jumps off the side tower, enters the acting area SR, crosses to centre and slams the drawbridge shut.

Why have you done this? He was mine!

He crosses to Esmé, taking the control in his hand and playing the scene on her level.

He was lost. And now he's found.

ESMÉ: No darling, now he's dead. In his mama's arms. Oh that must bring back a lot of memories for you!

Ronnie kneels, grabs Esmé by the throat and lifts her straight up to his eye level.

JESUS: Don't you dare!

They are eye to eye for a moment. He slowly puts the marionette down again.

I gave my blood for you.

ESMÉ: I wonder how much I could get for a pint of that.

JESUS: It's not for sale.

ESMÉ: Oh please! The world has been paying the price for your blood for far too long.

JESUS: I gave it freely.

ESMÉ: Look sweetie, that myth may wash with the desperate and discouraged, but I don't buy it. You should stay down here with these people for awhile. You won't be crowned in glory. You'll be covered in dirt and shit and blood.

JESUS: It's not time.

ESMÉ: Well, don't wait too long. Comebacks get harder the longer you wait, believe me. And look, there's your cross.

He picks up the cross.

JESUS: What is this, Esmé?

ESMÉ: Home sweet home.

JESUS: Stop it.

ESMÉ: What's the matter? Don't you recognise it?

He throws the cross down.

JESUS: I said stop.

ESMÉ: That's it, isn't it? Oh I know that most of your history was rewritten to serve the scare tactics of Rome, but you never really died on the cross, did you?

JESUS: What are you saying?

ESMÉ: You are a liar. An illegitimate bastard who invented a fantasy life for himself to protect his whore mother!

JESUS: I'm warning you!

ESMÉ: What's the matter, darling? Finding it hard to turn the other cheek?

JESUS: I died on the cross.

ESMÉ: Liar.

JESUS: I rose again.

ESMÉ: Liar.

JESUS: I am sanctuary. I am forgiveness. I am love.

ESMÉ: You are a liar!

JESUS: What do you want?!

ESMÉ: Proof.

JESUS: Of what?

ESMÉ: Your splendid pain.

JESUS: I can't. Not again.

ESMÉ: Show me.

JESUS. Once. He said just once.

ESMÉ: Show me.

He lifts the cross and holds it, remembering.

JESUS: I was all alone up there. That's why I appear, one at a time. I know the longing. I know the loneliness.

ESMÉ: I want to know your pain. Let me drink from your holy cup.

She crawls onto him. As the following seduction becomes more intimate, her mouth gets closer to his neck.

JESUS: You want my pain?

ESMÉ: Yes.

JESUS: You want my suffering?

ESMÉ: Yes.

JESUS: You want my blood?

ESMÉ: Yes darling. Give it to me.

JESUS: Then know it. And to hell with you!

He raises the cross and violently thrusts it into her. Shrill music/sound sting. Red light fills the area.

ESMÉ: Why?!

JESUS: Now you know my pain. And you are free.

Esmé dies, her control thrown to the floor. Ronnie leans and kisses her on the lips. He then holds the cross in front of him, clasps each side with his hands and stares into the audience.

Fine. I'm back.

Music begins, as Ronnie thrusts upward. The SM is above on the SL bridge and takes the rising cross from his hands as the "Techno Jesus" sound and light show begins again. Ronnie clears Esmé and hangs her backstage R. He climbs back up on the bridge level and he and the SM position three rolled up quilt panels on each bridge leaning rail. Music changes. Lighting rebuilds to a daytime wash. Edna #4 enters from the alley entrance SL of the centre bridge tower. She is dressed in a hat and coat, carrying her purse.

EDNA: I haven't slept in days. Needed to finish my quilt. Needed it to be done and out of my hands. But I feel good. I feel calm. Okay dear, let 'er rip.

The SM unties two cords on the SL leaning rail and a quilt panel unrolls, covering the entire area from the leaning rail to the deck floor. The centre of the panel reads "Stanley Rural, 1924—1986". There is a cloth appliqué of a plate of bacon and eggs.

This is for my Stanley. My bacon and eggs man. A remembrance panel in honour of his life. Hung here for all of Turnip Corners to see.

She begins to cross to SR.

The whole quilt was supposed to be for Stanley. I guess I figured if I made it so big that it would never be finished, then I would never have to acknowledge why it was being made in the first place. But life had another plan, and I had to cut it into a manageable size. I had to hang my quilt up for everyone to see. And if they don't like it, or can't deal with it, or if it makes them angry, well then, as Eden would have said, fuck them.

The SM unties another panel on the SR bridge leaning rail. It reads "Eden Urbane, 1957—2001". There is a cloth appliqué of musical notes.

This is for my Eden. I wasn't sure how best to tell the world about him. He was a complex boy. Man. But those notes are music that he loved. The beginning of the chorus to "Midnight in Monte Carlo".

She softly sings:

All I remember
Is midnight and moonlight
You're but a ghost in the mist...
My Edie. He always loved this purse.

She walks toward CS.

So here I am, flanked by my men. And forever a part of them. It was a long time in the making, but we were...no, we *are* the Rural family.

Ronnie unties a third quilt panel which unrolls directly behind Edna CS. It reads "Edna Rural, 1927—?" There is a cloth appliqué of a fork sewn onto the centre of the quilt, shadowed by the familiar red AIDS ribbon symbol.

Yes, I made my own panel. Can't assume that anyone else will acknowledge how I die, much less care.

Turnip Corners is a funny place that way. It's a hard town to be positive in, if you catch my drift. And lord love a duck, who would care about an HIV-positive old biddy in a Sears housedress anyway!

Special up on Ronnie's face.

JESUS: I do.

Edna turns and looks up.

EDNA: I know that. Now. Thanks for appearing in my quilt, Jesus.

JESUS: Thank you for recognising me, Edna. I hope the road is clearer now.

EDNA: Oh, I don't know if it's any clearer, dear, but at least I know which direction I'm headed in. When you see your mum, tell her I think she should be very proud of you.

The light fades out on Ronnie.

I always thought that when my quilt was done, it would be finished. But I don't think that's true, necessarily. Eventually, hopefully, someone will take that big question mark off of my panel and replace it with a date. I could have left it blank, I suppose, but somehow that question mark is reassuring to me. A great big sign saying, "Well Edna, what's it going to be? What sweet adventure will you take today?"

So I'm going to dance while the music is still playing. And I won't worry if there's no one to dance with. I'm going to turn the TV off and look at things in three dimensions. I'm going to switch off the radio and listen to my own thoughts. I'm going to take a nap in the middle of the day and not feel guilty about it. I'm going to call up Don Divine and ask him for a date. I'm going down to the Red Lantern Café and have myself a plate of french fries for supper. And I'm saving room for dessert, because this time, I'm going to have a slice of the pie!

Fluffer appears in the entrance alley just left of the CS bridge.

FLUFFER: Mrs. Rural!

EDNA: Oh, Fluffer dear, don't you look pretty today!

FLUFFER: Oh, thanks, Mrs. Rural. Hey, we got a postcard from Mr. Bishop!

EDNA: Oh Spanky! How's he doing?

FLUFFER: Well, he lost Miss Häagen-Daz in Montréal, but he made it to Ottawa and he says he's never eaten better in his life.

EDNA: Good for him. I hope he gets to dine at 24 Sussex.

FLUFFER: I've got Eden's Monte Carlo loaded with all the gear Mrs. Rural. We'd better shake a leg if we're gonna make the show on time.

EDNA: Thank you, Fluffer dear. I'll just say my good-byes.

FLUFFER: I'll wait in the car Mrs. Rural.

EDNA: Fluffer, when we're in public, I think you should call me by my stage name dear.

FLUFFER: Sure thing...Miss Edna Urbane!

Fluffer exits.

EDNA: Well, I'd best be off. I've taken over Eden's Karaoke Memory Lane business, and Fluffer and I got ourselves a gig at a hospice in the city. Oh I know, I'm just a silly old biddy. But I think it'll work out just fine. And if there's one thing I am, it's positive.

SFX of car horn.

Did you hear that? It's life calling me again. Wish me luck, dears, and remember, no matter what happens to you, keep your fork, because I guarantee...there's pie.

Alright, Winnie dear, you can play us out now.

Music in, a piano version of "Behold, The Blessed Prairie". Edna exits as acting area light fades, leaving a special on the fork motif of the centre quilt panel. Ronnie crosses to the SL side tower, picks up a miniature blue Monte Carlo and attaches it to a string running along the "highway" atop the US puppet hanging rail. The SM, on the SR side tower, begins to pull the string, causing the car to "drive" in front of the US prairie horizon. Music swells and the horizon glows as Ronnie waves goodbye. Black.

The End